PRIEST

TED WOODS

To Sue.

Hope you enjoy

Ted.

Beaten Track
www.beatentrackpublishing.com

Priest

First published 2021 by Beaten Track Publishing
Copyright © 2021 Ted Woods

Paperback ISBN: 978 1 78645 524 6
eBook ISBN: 978 1 78645 525 3

Cover photos:
St. Peter's Church, Formby; taken by David Holroyd.

Beaten Track Publishing,
Burscough, Lancashire.
www.beatentrackpublishing.com

For my wife, Anne, with love and thanks, and in memory of David Wilkinson, a wonderful organist, colleague and friend.

Thanks also to Debbie McGowan of Beaten Track Publishing for her advice and support.

Chapter 1

Look, Wendy, shit happens!" Paula said. "Even in the church...maybe especially in the church! I know ideally it shouldn't, but it does."

Wendy Morris, the rector of St. Olaf's church, had come home after a particularly trying meeting and had phoned her friend, Paula Armstrong, also a rector, for a chat and a moan. They had been friends since their Theological College days and phoned each other most weeks.

"I remember my first boss telling me that there are probably seven people who are replicated in every church, and identifying them early on is the key," Paula told Wendy. "You've got the stubborn, the bossy, the 'won't listen' and the 'I'm right'. And let me tell you from bitter experience, these are the ones who take up a disproportionate amount of time."

"There are more?" Wendy asked nervously.

"Yes, but the final three are the ones who make it all worthwhile—the willing, the encourager and the 'I'll have a go'."

"I have some of the last three here in St. Olaf's, but the problem is they never open their mouths when you need them to! Anyway, Paula, thanks. It's just that I had a rather shitty meeting tonight and needed to offload it. As the hymn says, I'll 'fight the good fight with all my might'!"

Paula laughed. "I prefer what one minister in John Major's government was once told—'Don't let the buggers get you down!' I'm afraid shitty meetings happen! Don't I know! Speak soon!"

In fact, the whole evening had been a bit of a disaster. First, Wendy was running late for the monthly Select Vestry meeting. A parishioner had died, and their family had rung to tell her and to begin make some tentative arrangements for the funeral. She couldn't really cut them off even though she was short of time.

And then, as she rushed up the corridor of the parish hall to the committee room, she overheard voices in the kitchen and stopped to listen.

"She probably won't allow the matter to be taken," said one voice. "But we'll keep pressing it."

"And we'll back you up! At least the subject will be aired, and we'll have put her on the spot," said the second voice.

"We'd better not sit together. It might look pre-planned," said the third. "Which, of course, it is!" He laughed.

"OK! Give these cups a rinse and let's go. It's nearly time for the meeting to begin."

Wendy recognised all three voices as Vestry members. She walked quickly up the corridor, her footsteps silent on the carpet tiles.

They got through the agenda quickly and peaceably enough. It was all the usual stuff—finance, repairs, a new hoover. The purchase of a hoover took a bit of time, as everyone had an opinion. Sometimes in Select Vestries, it's easier to spend €100,000 than €100!

The end of the agenda. Wendy began gathering her papers before the closing prayer.

"Eh, before you close, Rector, I'd just like to mention something that we, I mean, I have heard some people talking about and that we should deal with." It was Edgar Broadstairs, one of the voices she had heard in the kitchen.

"You know, Edgar, I don't do 'Any Other Business' at meetings. If you want something raised, then you send it to the honorary secretary before the next agenda is sent out."

"But it's a matter of urgency," Edgar went on, determined to have his say. "We're losing a lot of our young people to St. Stephen's because, well, they are much more modern in their approach than we are. Guy Morgan is a really super rector. Very clued in to what young people want."

"I agree!" It was Raymond Johnson, the second voice in the kitchen. "All the young people are going there. You really need to up your game, Rector, if you don't mind me saying so."

Well, actually, I do mind you saying so, thought Wendy.

And then the third voice, that of Sam Davidson, piped up, "I think we should set up a committee to look at how we can modernise our services. Maybe we need to think of starting up a music band to jazz up the hymns like they do in St. Stephen's. Mr. Finch, the school principal, has offered to help. He's very involved with their new music group."

Ah, so that's who's behind this. Laurence Finch. Relations had soured between the school principal and Wendy of late. Laurence Finch was not someone who could forgive and forget if he was crossed, and Wendy knew, after a few run-ins with the principal, given any opportunity, he would stir up trouble for her.

The rest of the Vestry members stayed mute.

"Liturgy and services are my responsibility," Wendy said evenly. "I'm open to suggestions, and you can speak to me anytime, but they are not in the Select Vestry's remit to discuss."

"Well, you're going to lose a lot of young people—and young families. We don't want that to happen in St. Olaf's. Don't say we didn't warn you."

"My door is always open," said Wendy. "Now, let us stand and say the Grace."

As Wendy was putting her papers away, one of the churchwardens, Jim O'Keeffe, came over to her. "That was out of order. I'm glad you didn't give them the opportunity to develop their hare-brained ideas. You handled them very well."

"Yes," said Carol Watkins, a member of the choir. "What a stupid thing to suggest! Next, they'll want to do away with the organ and the choir! We can't let that happen. Well done for stopping them!"

But none of you spoke up, thought Wendy. A little bit of support would have been welcome.

Wendy drove back to the rectory. The streetlamp outside the gates was still broken. There were no lights on the long driveway, and in her rush to get to the Select Vestry meeting, she had forgotten to put on any outside lights. The house was wreathed in darkness and not looking very inviting.

Opening the front door by the light of her mobile phone, she went to the kitchen, made a cup of coffee and rang Paula. She needed to let off some steam before she went to bed. Otherwise, she wasn't going to be able to sleep.

That was one of the disadvantages of being single and in charge of a parish: when Wendy came home after a difficult day, there was no one to sound off to.

Chapter 2

S T. OLAF'S RECTORY was built in the 1960s. Unlike many modern clergy houses, it had not been built in the grounds of the original rectory, although it looked as if it might have been.

The big house on the left-hand side of the driveaway was called Chalfont and had belonged to the Loftus family, the owners of the local flour mill. A high wall and impressive wrought iron gates hid the house from the road outside, separating the Loftus family socially as well as physically from the local inhabitants of Lislea. The original rectory had been closer to the town—and to the church—but as a large, three-storey house over a basement, it had been deemed too expensive to maintain and heat.

True, the old rectory had an attractive Georgian front door, complete with stained-glass fanlight and an imposing set of steps up to it, but there the attraction ended. The windows were draughty, the ceilings were high, the rooms too big, and the cellar was damp and unusable.

The mill owner, Stanley Loftus, was on the Select Vestry of St. Olaf's when a replacement rectory was being discussed, and to save the parish unnecessary expense in having to buy a new plot, he offered a site for a new rectory in part of the extensive grounds of Chalfont. The site he offered was furthest away from the house and had been the piggery, but no matter. It was being given for free, and the Select Vestry were not going to look a gift pig in the mouth! All they asked was that Mr. Loftus add the piece of land between the piggery and the road to provide an entrance and a garden.

This was agreed on two conditions. First, that a high wall, the same height as the existing wall that fronted Chalfont, would be built between the rectory site and the grounds of Chalfont, and second, that trees would be planted to hide the wall from Chalfont's side. The entrance gate to the rectory was situated where the street-side high wall of Chalfont ended, and a sixty-yard driveway followed the new wall to the front of the rectory.

The hall door of the rectory faced the high wall. The trees had grown so tall over the years that they now kept the sun off that side of the house, and the tarmac in front of the house was always covered in moss. But on the other side of the rectory was a bright and spacious garden which had been planted with flowers and shrubs, shielded from the road by an equally high wall.

The Loftus family no longer lived in Chalfont. A year or two before Wendy had arrived in St. Olaf's, Stanley's widow had died and the family decided that since their milling business had moved to Daneford, they would sell the property. It wasn't on the market for long, but the new owners were something of a mystery.

Shortly after the purchase, a new sign on the front gates announced that it had become 'The Chalfont Institute', the headquarters of a group specialising in 'treating' disabled children, but locals noticed that very few cars went in or out. The impressive gates were now electronically operated, so the new owners and those who visited didn't have to get out of their cars to enter the property.

It all added to the mystery of the place.

The previous incumbent told Wendy that when his children accidentally kicked their balls over the high wall into Chalfont, they never got them back.

The people of Lislea had their own theories about the new owners of Chalfont, the most common being that it was a front for some dubious or illegal business.

Wendy could see the house from the landing window. Lights came on in the evening, but no one was ever seen.

At least she had neither nosey nor noisy neighbours, and that suited her just fine. But she could do with some security lighting, especially in winter.

Chapter 3

LAURENCE FINCH, THE principal of St. Olaf's Primary School, was not a man to fall out with. Any disagreement, however well-intentioned and reasoned, was taken as a personal insult. Those who didn't agree with him were enemies, only out to undermine his authority and therefore to be resisted and rubbished. He never forgot, and he never forgave.

The Revd. Wendy Morris, as rector of the parish, was chair of the school board of management, as well as having a pastoral role in the school.

Of late, her relations with the principal had been arctic. They had differed over accounting for funds raised for the school. Then there had been a row over the admission of a child with a learning disability and, just recently, there had been a dispute over extracurricular activities, and Wendy's neutral stance had been twisted by Laurence Finch into collusion with disaffected parents to challenge his authority as principal.

There had been some tense meetings not only with the principal, who insisted that a union official be present, but also with her archdeacon, Guy Morgan. Laurence Finch had reported Wendy to the bishop about her perceived lack of support for the school and himself, and the bishop had sent his archdeacon to bring Wendy into line. Laurence Finch was also a member of the archdeacon's congregation and a great supporter of all that Guy Morgan was doing at nearby St. Stephen's. The odds were stacked against Wendy from the start.

Never a person to let things be, Laurence Finch was determined to get revenge and make things difficult for Wendy. As principal of the parish school, he had many contacts in St. Olaf's, whom he used to criticise how Wendy was running her parish.

"It's none of my business, I know, not being a parishioner of St. Olaf's, but did you know that a lot of your young people have started attending St. Stephen's? Our rector, Guy Morgan, is really pulling them in. It's quite the place to go on Sunday evenings, what with all the new facilities he has built. I know you think your rector is good...but I'm only saying."

He knew who to pick for these conversations: people who hadn't got their way or who had disagreed with some of Wendy's decisions, and even some, paradoxically, who didn't like the child-friendly services that Wendy had introduced.

"If I were on your Select Vestry, I'd bring it up," he'd say to those he knew were members, among them the 'three amigos' who had met in the kitchen of the parish hall before the last Vestry meeting.

One of them was Edgar Broadstairs, who fancied himself as an expert on church music. He had sung in cathedral choirs as a boy and later as a tenor but considered the church choir in St. Olaf's not good enough for his talent. He was more than a little peeved that Wendy had overlooked his great musical gifts and had not taken him up on his offer to become 'Director of Music', which would have meant picking the hymns and music for Sunday services and overseeing the organist.

Raymond Johnson was annoyed that Wendy had not only increased the frequency of parish communions but had also dropped some of the canticles from morning prayer. An old-fashioned *Book of Common Prayer* devotee, he'd have them reciting the litany every month. He never attended church in the evenings, so was unconcerned about what kind of service might be put on for 'the youth'.

Thirdly, there was Sam Davidson, whose only principle was to take the opposite view in any debate, just to stir things up.

And these were the people who wanted a music group, complete with guitars and drums, introduced to St. Olaf's!

Chapter 4

IT WAS MONDAY morning. Edgar Broadstairs and Raymond Johnson sat down at their usual table at their usual time in Kate's Coffee Shop on Lislea's Main Street. They were joined, as usual, by the Revd. Canon William Allen, former rector of St. Olaf's and Wendy's immediate predecessor.

William Allen had been rector of St. Olaf's for over thirty years. Affable and easy-going, he had not been one for innovation or new projects and had kept St. Olaf's ticking over nicely. He let Laurence Finch run the school, always agreeing with the principal's decisions and letting him get on with things, which was the way Laurence liked it.

William's wife, Cecily, had been his partner in ministry. In fact, to get to William, people usually had to get past Cecily first, either on the phone or at the front door of the rectory.

Each night, before going to sleep, Cecily would quiz him about the day's happenings, telling him what he had got right—and wrong!

Among a closed circle of parishioners with whom they socialised, William used to joke, "I'm the rector, but Cecily is the director!"

A few years before he was due to retire, William was asked to make a special visit to Dr. Philip Darling, one of his parishioners who was a retired doctor. The doctor was a widower, without any children, and a big supporter of the church.

"I thought you should know that I will shortly be leaving Lislea," he informed William after some initial chit-chat.

"My younger brother has asked me to go and live with him and his wife in England. They have just moved into a house with a self-contained annexe. He says it would suit me down to the ground. I've always got on well with him and his wife, and their children live nearby. Now that I'm retired, it would be nice to be near them while also having my own space."

"Yes, I can understand that," said William. "As you know, Cecily and I have no children either, and we often wonder what we will do when I retire."

"And that's what I want to talk to you about," said the doctor. "I've been thinking of this house and what I should do with it. Neither my brother nor I are short of money, and the thought occurred to me that I should perhaps leave this house to the Church for the use of retired clergy, with clergy from St. Olaf's being offered it first."

"That's extremely generous of you. I think it is a wonderful idea," said William. "As you know, in the Church of Ireland, retirement housing is the responsibility of each clergyperson, and with the way house prices have risen, few can afford anything around this area because of its proximity to Dublin. They have to move far away from friends and all that is familiar.

"I know of a few houses that have been given to the Church, and I know how well it works. It would be greatly appreciated and take a load of worry off many clergy who have not been able to buy a house for their retirement. Can I thank you most sincerely for your generosity and thoughtfulness?"

They talked some more about the details, and William advised Dr. Darling to get in touch with the legal department in Church House.

The doctor's house was not far from the rectory, and within a few minutes, William was back home.

"I've got great news!" he declared to Cecily. "Philip Darling is moving to England to be with his brother, and he's leaving his house to the Church, for retired clergy. And clergy from St. Olaf's get first refusal!"

"What a godsend!" said Cecily, sitting down. "God does work in mysterious ways!"

What to do about retirement had been the subject of many conversations between William and Cecily, and it was a great worry as the years went by. They didn't own any property, and the rectory went with the job. Their savings were modest: getting a mortgage wasn't going to happen at their age, and rent around Lislea was more than they could afford.

But now, thanks to Dr. Darling, they would be able to stay among the friends and acquaintances they had known for years. And sure, wouldn't he and Cecily be a great asset for his successor!

As soon as the house became available, William retired and moved into it, and every Monday morning, he held court in Kate's Coffee Shop with some of his former parishioners to keep up to date with the gossip and to pass judgement on his successor.

Chapter 5

WHILE WILLIAM ALLEN enjoyed his coffee and chat, his wife Cecily stood at the supermarket checkout, confused and mortified. A queue stretched out behind her as she tried to remember the PIN of her bank card.

Was it 4692 or 4269? She entered the first combination, but it was rejected. She tried the other number, but it didn't work either. She could sense the impatience of the people behind her.

"Perhaps I can just sign the slip this time?" she anxiously asked the cashier. "I mean, before it gobbles up my card."

The girl at the checkout rang for her supervisor. People began to shuffle off to other queues. Cecily's face was red with embarrassment.

She knew she had the number written in a little black book— somewhere back in the house. It had been coded into a telephone number, and it would take some time, and quiet, to work out whether her four-digit PIN was at the front, middle or end of the fictitious phone number.

The supervisor was understanding, took the details of her card and got her to sign a slip. Cecily gathered her shopping and headed for her car.

Next problem. Where had she parked the car? And it had started to rain!

Lately, Cecily had begun to worry at the way names and numbers just seemed to pop out of her head. Whereas when they lived in the rectory, she had an immediate recall of numbers, birthdays and anniversaries, who said what, when and where, since William's retirement, there were times when her mind just went blank and she couldn't recall a person's name or, as had just happened, her PIN.

Events that happened years ago, even in childhood, she could recall with clarity and accuracy, but what she did last week, or even yesterday, was another matter altogether.

She had also begun to mislay things. Throughout William's ministry, she had been the organised one, checking his diary, making sure he went to meetings on time and saw the people he had promised to visit.

Only the other day, her friend, Glenda, had rung to confirm the time she would collect her for their monthly 'ladies' lunch', and Cecily had forgotten all about it and wasn't ready when Glenda called.

And the mobile phone! It was driving her to distraction. She had mastered texting, still putting in full words and punctuation. But whatever button she had pressed, it was now on predictive text and she didn't know how to cancel it.

After finding her car and depositing her shopping, she decided to try and get her mobile sorted in one of the phone shops in the sprawling shopping centre.

She was met by an assistant—a young lad who couldn't have been more than eighteen! Of course, you had to be young to know about mobile phones.

"How can I help you?" he asked pleasantly.

She took out her phone. "It's doing all sorts of funny things when I try to text. I just can't cope with…" Her mind went blank. "I think it's called protected sex!" The young man blushed. And then she remembered. "Oh, no! I meant predictive text!" Now it was her turn to blush.

Where was it all going to end? She wouldn't tell William because it would only worry him. But whatever it was, it was getting worse.

Chapter 6

FOLLOWING THE FATAL car accident in which Bishop Arthur Easterby and his wife, Sarah, died, Daneford diocese was vacant again.

The police were still searching for Lily MacDonald, the housekeeper at the See House and their chief suspect, but Lily seemed to have disappeared, and the case had gone cold.

Not only in Daneford, but throughout the Church of Ireland, speculation was once again rife about a possible successor.

A number of the laity, led by Laurence Finch, were mobilising behind Daneford's archdeacon, The Ven. Guy Morgan, who was 'packing them in' in St. Stephen's. Guy had been brought over from England by Bishop Easterby to spearhead a Growth and Renewal agenda in the diocese and had been quickly promoted to be archdeacon—much to the disgust of some of the longer-serving clergy in the diocese. Guy was popular with the laity, but the clergy were not enamoured with their new archdeacon and all the statistics he demanded, the seminars he expected them to attend and his yearly reviews of their work as parish priests.

Each year, he had a morning session with each cleric to review their ministry, during which he would ask, "What has gladdened you in the past year? What has saddened you? What's your golden ticket? And how are you going to make it happen?"

The clergy were getting tired of this annual interrogation by the archdeacon, and while they valued a listening ear *when* they needed one, they found Guy's irrepressible optimism, the 'super' with which he peppered his conversation and his habit of recounting how he had successfully dealt with similar problems, had become frankly annoying.

They had nicknamed him *I, Guy!*

Without the support of the clergy, Guy had little chance of being elected bishop of Daneford, and slowly, a consensus formed that perhaps the best solution was a translation, i.e., the appointment of someone who was already a bishop and who would have the experience to help the diocese get over its sense of shock at the Easterbys' murder, for that is what the police called it.

That, in the end, is what happened. Even though he had just six years to go before retirement, the Rt. Revd. Christopher Hawkesworth was elected and confirmed as the new bishop of Daneford.

Christopher Hawkesworth was regarded as 'a safe pair of hands'. He had served all his ministry in the Church of Ireland with both rural and urban experience. He had been an archdeacon and the dean of a major cathedral before being elected a bishop ten years ago. Well respected, a moderate, both theologically and liturgically, he was just the person to take over Daneford in the wake of Arthur Easterby's tragic death.

The clergy of Daneford were pleased. Christopher Hawkesworth was known to be fair. He was also a bishop who kept in touch with his clergy, often inviting himself to rectories and curatages for a lunchtime bowl of soup and a chat, just to hear how his clergy and their families were. He also had a reputation of making sure that rectories were generously prepared for incoming clergy.

Rectories were a nightmare for some clergy. Having been appointed to a parish, they then had to negotiate the refurbishment of their tied house with glebewardens who had probably not been involved in the appointment process. The glebewardens invariably wanted to spend as little money as possible on the rectory, and it was not unknown for some clergy to withdraw from an appointment due to an impasse in negotiations.

The nominators who made the appointment could, and usually did, make sympathetic noises. But some were not even on the Select Vestry, which ultimately made the decision on how much, or how little, should be done, and two mean glebewardens and a miserly treasurer were a formidable trio for a new incumbent to deal with. Few new appointees wanted to start their ministry in a new parish with a row over the rectory—something the new bishop would, hopefully, prevent happening.

Chapter 7

Another, if lesser, vacancy had to be filled in Daneford diocese—St. Saviour's, Lislea.

In the early days of the late and not entirely lamented bishop, Arthur Easterby, St. Saviour's had become vacant, and the nominators, led by veteran ecclesiocrat, Harry White, had been keen on a cleric in a neighbouring diocese.

Arthur had stalled and stymied the appointment. The Revd. Steve Adams was not a card-carrying evangelical and had even asked questions about the Growth and Renewal agenda in General Synod. In Arthur's mind, he was not the kind of cleric he wanted in Daneford. He preferred clones of himself and the archdeacon, Guy Morgan. Arthur had been planning to start the process of making an appointment to St. Saviour's in the New Year, but his fatal accident had intervened.

As an engineer who gave a lot of time and service to the Church of Ireland, not just in Daneford, Harry White was well-known and respected in Church circles and had sat on central committees with many of the bishops, including Christopher Hawkesworth, who had often consulted him on difficult to resolve architectural matters.

Harry decided to approach the new bishop about Steve Adams and St. Saviour's.

"My fellow nominators were in agreement that Steve Adams was, and still is, the person for St. Saviour's. He's done a very good job in his present parish, where he has been for eight years.

We did approach him about applying, and he was considering it when your predecessor pulled the plug."

"Umm." Bishop Hawkesworth was not going to discuss his predecessor, however much he disagreed with Arthur Easterby's managerial model of episcopacy. "But Mr. Adams will have to apply in the usual way."

"Of course," said Harry. "With your permission, we'd like to get in touch with him again, in case he moves elsewhere. It has been known to happen."

"I've heard good reports about him, and he would be an asset in the diocese. I'll get the process of advertising the parish again into motion, and we'll take it from there."

After a few pleasantries, Harry left the See House, well pleased with himself.

Having informed his fellow nominators of his meeting with the bishop, he sat down to ring Steve Adams.

"Hello, Steve. This is Harry White from St. Saviour's."

**

"Ye-es?" replied Steve, not sure what to expect.

"You know how disappointed we were that our previous bloody bishop…oops, sorry, I mustn't speak ill of the dead! But I told you he stalled the appointment process until it ran out of time. Well, I spoke to our new bishop today, and he's going to advertise St. Saviour's again. He thinks highly of you. So, I hope you're still open to applying."

Steve was caught unawares. The talk with the nominators and the subsequent visit to St. Saviour's had been very unsettling. He had tried to put it to bed, but every now and again, he found himself wondering *what if…?*

It was a fantasy game he enjoyed playing, but now it was a real possibility once again.

"Uh, well, eh," he stumbled. "I had put it completely out of my mind," he lied. "Let me have a chat with Fiona and give it some more thought, and I'll come back to you."

"Well, I certainly hope you will," enthused Harry. "The other nominators and I think you are the right person for St. Saviour's, and if you agree to apply, you will have our fullest backing. And remember, we will put the rectory right for you and Fiona. That's a promise!"

***

Steve was sitting at his desk, frowning and staring into space, when his wife, Fiona, walked in with a cup of coffee.

Seeing his troubled face, she asked, "Who was that on the phone? It must have been bad news by the look on you!"

"I don't know if it's bad news or not," replied Steve. "That was Harry White from St. Saviour's. They want me to apply again. And the bishop is apparently quite keen, too."

Chapter 8

As if WENDY Morris hadn't enough on her hands with the school problems and Laurence Finch's recent meddling in parish affairs, her father had been diagnosed with Alzheimer's.

Wendy had a brother who lived in Dublin. He ran his own financial advisory business and was under a lot of pressure. He was married and had three school-going children, which put extra demands on him, as his wife also ran her own beauty parlour. When he wasn't working, he was ferrying the children around and trying to do his share at home. His visits to his parents were sporadic, and he was happy to let, indeed expected, Wendy to keep in touch with their mother and father.

"You're single with no family responsibilities, and sure, you only work one day a week!"

Truth to tell, Wendy's brother was finding it hard to accept his father had Alzheimer's and felt guilty when he saw how harassed his mother looked.

On her day off, Wendy went home to see her parents. Her father's farm was now rented out, and this provided her mother with a reasonable income.

"I'll try to keep your father at home and look after him for as long as I can," her mother said. "But it's not getting any easier. He wanders a lot and gets all sorts of strange ideas about what's going on. In fact, he's become quite paranoid. He thinks neighbours are out to get him or cheat him out of the farm. And that's worrying me, not least because he keeps a rifle in the gun cabinet in the hall. The other day, he was turning out drawers looking for the key. I've hidden it, but what if he finds it some day when I'm out? He'd be a danger to himself—and to others."

Her mother paused and looked at Wendy. "It's a lot to ask, but could you take that rifle and put it somewhere safe in the rectory? I'd ask your brother, but he's got children. I know guns and clergy don't go together, but I would be so relieved to have it out of the house. We can decide what to do with it later."

So it was that Wendy found herself driving back to Lislea with a rifle and some boxes of cartridges covered by an old rug in the boot of her car. She kept religiously within the speed limit, praying she wouldn't be stopped by the police.

She could imagine the headlines in the local paper—*Shootin', Tootin' Vicar, Wendy Morris!*

Arriving back after dark, she opened her front door and went back for her bundle in the boot. The house phone rang. Wendy dumped the rifle and cartridges in the cubby hole under the stairs and went into her study to take the call. It was the honorary secretary of the Select Vestry checking on some details before sending out the minutes, followed by a good old rant about the antics of the three amigos, as they had now become known.

By the time she had rung off, all Wendy thought of was making a hot chocolate and going to bed. Usually, she would ring Paula for a chat, but she was too tired and needed a sleep.

Chapter 9

N OT HAVING TO go to an evening meeting for a change, Steve suggested to Fiona that they take their cups of coffee into his study, where it was less likely their children, Laura and Andrew, would overhear them discussing what to do about St. Saviour's.

"I'm just getting used to staying in St. Patrick's after that mess about a move to St. Saviour's," said Fiona as they sat on the sofa in the corner of his office.

"Me too," replied Steve.

"What is it now? Six months?"

"Yeah, and now it's all up in the air again. I suppose I could just say no and be done with it."

"I can hear a 'but' coming." Fiona raised her eyebrows.

"Harry White has spoken to the new bishop, who seems to think well of me—not like Arthur Easterby!"

"That bloody man!" Fiona muttered.

They rehearsed all the old arguments. St. Saviour's was a bigger parish than St. Patrick's. Steve had served eight years in St. Patrick's, had worked hard and had the parish running smoothly and well. But after eight years, it was time either to move or to get a new vision for where he was. He was not a person to tread water. St. Saviour's also had a curate, and Steve would enjoy working with and training a colleague.

"And Harry White has promised to see that the rectory is fully refurbished," he added.

Fiona thought back to their visit. The rectory had been a disaster zone. Evidence of the previous rector's amateurish DIY efforts were all over the house, down to homemade presses in the kitchen and bathroom. There wasn't even a proper oven, just an ancient solid stove augmented by a dual electric ring. The place felt damp and reeked of cigarette smoke. The bedrooms were huge, there was no en-suite, and the toilet was off a landing halfway down the stairs.

"Refurbishment!" snorted Fiona. "It needs knocking down and rebuilding!"

"Harry's an engineer," Steve pointed out. "He's promised us an input before any plans are finalised. But the big question is the children. Laura, in particular. Andrew's due to move school in September anyway, so moving to a new area may not be such a change. But Laura—well, you saw what her response was when we said a move might be on the cards."

Six months ago, fifteen-year-old Laura had not reacted well to a proposed move, and that was putting it mildly. She'd accused her father of being selfish and heartless, putting his wishes before his family, especially herself. They had tried to discuss it around the kitchen table, but Laura had stomped out, slamming the kitchen door so hard it shattered some of the glass panes.

Deep down, Fiona knew Steve was becoming restless, and at forty-two he wasn't even halfway through his ministry. If it wasn't St. Saviour's, it would be somewhere else. Although she loved being in St. Patrick's and had made many friends there, she knew they couldn't stay there forever.

"Look," she said, "let's not make any decisions now. Let's give it a few days and make a decision then."

Fiona noticed her husband's pleasant surprise at her suggestion. He'd have been expecting a more negative response from her. Now she saw in him a glimmer of hope that maybe St. Saviour's would be a reality after all.

Chapter 10

APOCRYPHAL STORIES ABOUND about the sometimes-fraught relationships between clergy and organists, with clergy changing hymns at the last minute and organists refusing to change tunes.

Wendy had such a relationship with her organist, Cedric Selby, who—Wendy thanked the Lord!—had handed in his notice and was just about to take up a position in a 'spiky' church in Dublin.

Warning bells had rung for Wendy even before she was appointed to St. Olaf's three years previously. Cedric Selby had called to see her a few weeks before her institution to ask about her policy on choosing hymns. Was she happy to leave hymns and music to him, as her predecessor had done? Surely, she would be so busy in her new parish that she would be glad not to have the extra work. Indeed, Cedric offered to compile services for weddings, funerals and special occasions. It had been such an enormous help to the previous rector!

Wendy realised it was 'now or never'.

"Thank you for your very kind offer," she'd said, "but I like, as far as possible, to match hymns with the themes of the readings and my sermon for each Sunday. I usually look over the readings a month in advance to have some idea of the themes coming up, and that's when I choose hymns to tie in with them. I won't leave hymn lists until the last minute. I'll make sure you have them at least a week in advance."

Cedric was not too pleased.

Wendy wasn't long in St. Olaf's when Cedric wanted to change choir practice from a Wednesday evening to before church on Sunday morning. "I'm having great difficulty in getting the choir together for a midweek practice," he told her after church one Sunday. "Very few turn up. So, I've decided that choir practice will be for thirty minutes on Sunday mornings, ending fifteen minutes before the service begins. It's my only chance of running over music with the choir."

But as Wendy was to find out when she visited choir members, their lack of attendance at choir practice was more to do with Cedric's caustic comments about their singing ability than their availability.

In the vestry after services with the churchwardens and herself, Cedric was free with his comments on Wendy's choice of hymns and which hymns would have been more suitable. He also quite liked to make 'helpful' suggestions about her sermons and how she conducted worship.

Another bone of contention, which predated Wendy, was that Cedric refused to play for school services. He wouldn't demean himself playing silly jingles like 'Who's the King of the Jungle?' and 'If I Were a Butterfly'!

With Cedric declining to play for school services, the principal Laurence Finch promptly asked a former school parent, Ian Wilson, who was an organist in a church outside Lislea, to play instead. When Wendy came to St. Olaf's, Ian had been playing for school services for a number of years, and Wendy enjoyed the enthusiasm with which he played, and he was always friendly and chatty after services. She envied the church that had him as their organist.

So, imagine Wendy's surprise when she received a phone call from Ian Wilson, asking for an appointment to see her.

"I've heard Cedric Selby is leaving St. Olaf's," he said, coming straight to the point as he met Wendy in the rectory. "I'd like to apply for the post of organist—that is, if it hasn't already been filled."

Wendy couldn't have been more thrilled. If there was anyone she could have chosen as organist for St. Olaf's, it would be Ian Wilson.

"No, we haven't filled the position," she said. "In fact, we haven't even got round to advertising it yet. But as the appointment of an organist is mine, I can tell you here and now that I would be very happy for you to have the job!"

"Well, it's just that I feel I need a change," said Ian. "The choir has dwindled where I am. They are mostly on the old side, and it's hard to get replacements. They're not up to singing special anthems anymore. I know some of your choir and I'm sure I would enjoy working with them."

"Cedric is due to leave at the end of the month," Wendy said. "How much notice do you have to give?"

They discussed dates and salary. Ian asked about how hymns were chosen and offered to collaborate with Wendy, if that was what she wished. They arranged a further meeting to thrash out details after Wendy had informed the Vestry and agreed the salary.

The appointment hadn't gone down well with Edgar Broadstairs. Not only had his musical knowledge about the choice of hymns been refused by Wendy, but now he had been cut out of appointing a new organist. He had been looking forward to being on an appointment panel and throwing his musical weight around.

Wendy was well aware of Edgar Broadstairs' ambitions in this regard, and how dashing them would add to his opposition of her as rector, but the appointment of an organist was hers to make, and it was too good an opportunity to miss appointing Ian Wilson.

Chapter 11

IN HIS EARLY sixties, Ian Wilson was the manager of a small nursing home on the outskirts of Daneford, a job quite different from the one he had pursued for most of his working life as a member of the Police Service of Northern Ireland.

Ian grew up in Northern Ireland and was in his teens when 'The Troubles' were beginning.

The Troubles first started as civil rights protest marches, but quickly, in the divided society of the North, they became sectarian and politically divisive. There had been violence surrounding the early marches, but it had been relatively minor. Loyalists and Republicans threw stones and bottles at each other, but usually the police succeeded in keeping them apart from serious interaction with each other.

But the sectarianism and the violence soon escalated.

In the area of West Belfast where Ian grew up, both sides began stockpiling guns and homemade bombs, and being anywhere near a riot risked being hit with a stray bullet, though that didn't stop local residents standing at their front doors to have a grandstand view of the action.

At Ian's school, near the interface between Loyalist and Republican areas, police and soldiers patrolled at the end of the school day to prevent clashes between pupils from Protestant and Catholic schools.

One of the Loyalist paramilitary groups was active in a new housing estate near where Ian lived. Perched on a hill, the estate had a clear view of a Republican area about half a mile away, but between the two areas ran a valley divided by a small river and overgrown with trees and scrub. The Loyalists were known to have gone down into the valley, discharge some of their guns, and then tell the residents of the estate that the Republicans were shooting at them. It was a ploy to demand protection money from the people of the estate. The brave few who refused to pay up were told, ominously, "When you are at work, we can't guarantee the safety of your home and family!" and that usually worked.

One Loyalist group approached Ian's church, near the estate, and asked to rent the parish hall 'for keep-fit classes'. The Church refused, afraid that it was an excuse for paramilitary training and for stockpiling weapons under the floor of the hall. From then on, there was a clear divide between the paramilitaries and the Church to the extent that anything the Church tried to do for the community was boycotted by the group. As soon as the Church set up a Citizen's Advice Bureau, the paramilitaries set up a rival office.

Nevertheless, on leaving school, Ian joined what was then The Royal Ulster Constabulary, determined to do his bit in preventing violence and loss of life and working for peace.

On a call-out to a domestic violence incident in a Republican area one night, he and his fellow officers were ambushed. A bogus call to the police was a common ploy to lure them into an area where they would be attacked.

Ian was in the passenger seat of the armoured Land Rover, and on reaching the address got out to approach the house. He hadn't gone a few steps when he was hit by a hail of bullets. His upper body was saved because he was wearing a bulletproof vest, but he was badly hit in one leg. He hadn't a chance.

As the shots rang out and Ian fell, his fellow officers pulled him into the Land Rover. The driver did a quick U-turn and rammed the accelerator to the floor as bullets pinged off their reinforced vehicle. Ian was bleeding profusely, and they headed to the nearby Royal Victoria Hospital, where he received emergency treatment and was kept in for three days.

It was, to say the least, a traumatic experience. Although he recovered well, Ian was left with a limp in his right leg.

The police offered to transfer him to a desk job, which he accepted and became a member of a team investigating the illegal businesses of paramilitary groups. There were many such illegal businesses going on in Northern Ireland like money laundering, fuel smuggling, counterfeiting, loan sharking, drug trafficking and running gambling dens.

When the RUC became the Police Service of Northern Ireland in 2001, Ian took the opportunity to retire. He had served in the police for nearly thirty years, and he was tired of the stress and strain of constantly having to check his car for booby traps and bombs, added to which, he regularly received death threats as a member of the squad investigating illegal activities. His two children had gone to college in England, and like many others, they stayed there after graduating rather than return to Northern Ireland.

The one thing that had kept him sane during those years in the police force was his love of music and the organ lessons he took in St. Anne's Cathedral in the heart of Belfast.

When he retired, Ian and his wife, Jane, decided it was time to leave Northern Ireland and its divided society. They moved to the relative quiet of Lislea, where he picked up a job managing a small nursing home. It supplemented his police pension nicely, and he was able to pursue his love of music by playing the organ in a church on the outskirts of the town.

Chapter 12

THIS CAN'T GO on! It's absolute chaos out there. We're losing valuable time, and we're paying for it, too!"

It was 7:50 p.m. on Tuesday evening. Wendy had just seen the last children of the Bible Club leave the parish hall and was heading back into the hall to help the leaders with tidying up before the Bowls Club arrived for their eight-p.m. session. It was a tight turnaround but the only arrangement that was possible in the crowded programme of the hall.

Not that the Bowls Club agreed. Edgar Broadstairs, the club captain, confronted Wendy at the door of the hall.

"We need to be able to start play at eight p.m.!" he spluttered angrily. "But the way things are going, we're only rolling out the mats at eight p.m., so it's ten past eight by the time we can actually start playing. When there's a match with a visiting team, that's not fair!"

Before Wendy could open her mouth, Edgar Broadstairs continued, "And we can hardly get into the car park, with all those parents picking up their children, blocking the entrance, talking to one another and not parking properly. This has to stop!"

"As you know, the hall is in much demand," Wendy said as evenly as she could. "I think you'll find that we end the Bible Club at twenty to eight. That means the children leave by quarter to eight, apart from a few who have to wait for their parents. The car park should be empty by ten to. We're doing the best we can.

The bowls can go on as late as you like, and," she reminded him, "you have the hall two nights a week. The Bible Club meets only once a week."

"Well, it's not good enough! It's embarrassing when visitors arrive to mayhem as children pour out of the hall."

"On the contrary," Wendy replied. "I've spoken to a few of your opposing teams and, looking at all the children, they say they would like to have a problem like that in their churches— even those from St. Stephen's!" Wendy was still smarting from Edgar Broadstairs' ambush at the last Vestry meeting.

"Have you been in their suite of halls?" Edgar retorted triumphantly. "They're so modern, so well finished, they're a pleasure to play bowls in. Talking of which, you're going to have to do something about the floor in our hall. The surface is so uneven we have to put down a layer of felt before we can lay the mats. And we're not getting any younger!"

"Are you coming in, Edgar?" It was Raymond Johnson, another of the three amigos. "We're ready to start playing and you're on next!"

"Just coming," Edgar shouted to Raymond. To Wendy, he said, "This will come up at the Bowls AGM. We pay a substantial rental for our use of the hall, and we must be treated fairly! Now if you don't mind, I have to start my game." He pushed rudely past her.

Wendy went back inside the hall, said hello to the members, who were clearly embarrassed by their captain's behaviour, and went back to the rectory for a much-needed cup of coffee. She would give Paula a ring and catch up with her friend and try not to moan too much about parish life and bowls clubs in particular.

Chapter 13

I F CECILY ALLEN was secretly worried about the onset of dementia, so too was her husband, William, who had noticed how increasingly forgetful and absent-minded she had become.

She often came back from the supermarket with only half of what she had planned to buy and more of what they didn't need, and he'd seen the scrapes and dents in the car. He was dreading having to tell her to give up driving. He knew what a scene she would make. She loved the independence and freedom driving gave her.

Only the other day she had come back from shopping saying that she had lost her bank card and he would have to come with her in future so they could use his card. But when he looked in her purse, the card was there.

It was getting worse. Meals were burnt because she'd put something in the oven and then go off and do something else, completely forgetting what was being cooked until the smoke alarm went off.

He wasn't sure that when she got up during the night she would come back to bed. It wasn't unusual for her to be in the kitchen making breakfast—at four a.m.!

It was taking its toll on him. He was beginning to show his age, and it meant that he didn't go out much, as he was afraid to leave her in the house alone.

How long could he keep looking after her? What if he became ill? They had no children to fall back on. There was just the two of them. Cecily had a sister, but she was in England and had a family of her own.

Some of William's contemporaries had moved into sheltered accommodation, using capital from selling their retirement house to cover the balance between their pensions and occasional grants and the cost of sheltered accommodation. But in one case, when the spouse had developed severe Alzheimer's, she had to move into a high dependency unit, and the cost was nearly three times her husband's church pension!

It just didn't bear thinking about, and anyway, the Allens had no house to sell.

The only thing, he decided, was to look after Cecily for as long as he could, but it wasn't easy. It was sapping all his energy, and he knew Cecily would hate his former parishioners knowing how forgetful she was becoming.

Chapter 14

IT WAS DECISION time in St. Patrick's rectory. Steve had to ring Harry White to let him know whether or not he was applying for St. Saviour's. Steve was keen to apply, but he also had to think about Fiona and the children.

"Let's go for a walk and then have lunch out," Steve suggested.

They put their dog, Barney, into the back of Steve's estate car and drove to the nearby hills where there was a walk through a forest park. They walked silently, hand in hand, along the path through the trees, while Barney explored the undergrowth.

"So," Fiona began, "what are the pros and cons about a move to St. Saviour's?"

"Well, how much longer do you think we should stay at St. Patrick's?"

"There you go! Why do you always answer a question with a question? It's such an annoying habit. Just tell me what you think!"

"I'm at a bit of a crossroads, really," Steve admitted. "After eight years in St. Patrick's, I've seen most of what I'd planned come to fruition. And, I suppose, the question is, do I stay and get a second wind and think how things can develop from here, or should I go and have a fresh challenge somewhere else?"

"More questions!" Fiona reminded him.

"OK! Well, all things being equal, I would like a new challenge. I'm in my early forties. I should have two more moves in me before

I retire. I just don't want to go to seed, which I could start doing if I stayed in St. Patrick's for too long. So, there you have it!"

"An answer, at last!" Fiona smiled, adding, "As if I hadn't guessed!"

"I know we've been over this ground so many times. I'd love to work with a curate, which St. Saviour's has always had. I feel St. Saviour's is at a cusp, wanting to move forwards and not start falling back. And they recognise that. Yes, I'd love to get stuck in, but…" Steve trailed off.

"But…?" Fiona prompted.

"Well, there's your job for a start."

Fiona was a physiotherapist. She reasoned, "Lislea is a big enough town. That shouldn't be a problem. And anyway, Dublin is within an easy, commutable distance, if I don't get a position in Lislea."

"Then there's Laura and Andrew," Steve said. "Andrew's not really the problem. He won't be with his pals if we move to Lislea, but he makes friends easily, and he'd love the sport. As for Laura—you saw how she reacted before."

"I think she'll be OK," said Fiona. "She's just finishing transition year, and she knows she's going to have start working hard if she's to get the points she needs to do medicine. Not all her friends are motivated about exams and getting good marks, so maybe it will be a blessing in disguise if she starts a new school. She probably knows that, and it will give her a reason to get out of the constant round of parties, not that she would admit it! No, Laura will be all right."

"And the final question is," Steve said, after a pause. "What about the rectory? Is it too much to take on?"

Fiona shrugged. "It all depends on whether Harry White is as good as his word. The garden will be great for Barney, and it looks reasonably well-kept. But the house itself…"

"We were promised an input," Steve reminded her. "Harry White admitted that a lot needs to be done to it."

"But do the rest of the Vestry think that way as well?" That was Fiona, at her practical and honest best.

"The other thing is that the new bishop, Christopher Hawkesworth, has a reputation for being a bit of a stickler about rectories being in good order before clergy move into them. According to some of his clergy, he has even deferred services of institution if, in his opinion, the rectory isn't fit for purpose."

By this time, they had walked back to the entrance to the park. They drove to a nearby pub which served decent food and had tables outside so they could bring Barney with them.

"So, what do you think?" Steve asked as Fiona examined the menu.

"Questions again!" laughed Fiona. "I think we should have a glass of wine and toast a future in Lislea!"

Chapter 15

W ENDY WAS WORKING at her desk when the phone rang.
"Wendy! Guy Morgan here! Would you be free for a little chat sometime soon?"

Remembering her last chat with the same archdeacon over the school and Laurence Finch, Wendy asked cautiously, "What about?"

"I'm working on a proposal to put to the bishop for the future of some suburban parishes. It was Arthur Easterby's idea, actually, but there are a few things I'd like your opinion on, as Lislea is one of the areas I was asked to consider. I think it would be better to have a chat over a cup of coffee than to talk over the phone. Are you free, say, tomorrow morning? I'll pop by about eleven?"

"Yes, that's OK."

"Super! See you then!" Guy rang off.

Now what's he up to? And what crackpot idea has he about Lislea? At least Wendy wouldn't have long to wait to find out.

***

"Ah, thanks, Wendy. Super!"

Guy took the coffee from her as he sat down in her study the following morning. She waited for him to go on.

"Yes, well, as I said on the phone, I've been mulling over a proposal for the future of the churches in Lislea and was wondering what you might think. I haven't yet mentioned it to Bishop Christopher. Let's say, this is just an exploratory chat, but an urgent one at that."

"Why is that?" asked Wendy.

"The bishop is just about to re-advertise St. Saviour's. Bishop Arthur hadn't got round to making an appointment before he… well, before that tragic accident. One of the things Bishop Arthur was keen on was to streamline parishes in a particular area, to cut down on duplication, to make them more efficient, to make them more missional. I suppose you could call them 'team parishes'.

"In a way it's a kind of development of team ministries," Guy went on enthusiastically. "Instead of, say in our area of Lislea, three parishes all duplicating ministries and administrations, we could come together and share specialist ministries, and indeed, the burden of administration. Though, of course," he added, "each parish would still be independent and have their own Select Vestry."

"Can you spell that out in a little more detail?" asked Wendy.

"Well, for example, we could have a full-time administrator looking after all three parishes—their accounts, their payments, dealing with tax rebates and all official correspondence with the diocese. A full-time administrator could serve each Select Vestry and look after faculty applications, safeguarding protocols, insurance of buildings, quinquennial inspections and keep us up to date on new Church policies."

"That seems quite a 'super' job for one person," Wendy replied, although the irony of the description was lost on Guy.

"Yes. He or she would need some secretarial assistance," Guy admitted. "But it would all be centralised and unified."

Alarm bells were ringing in Wendy's head.

Guy continued, "It's just that before an appointment is made to St. Saviour's, that could be written into the parish profile."

"What you're talking about is a shared ministry team covering the three churches?"

"Yes, that's it. Instead of us all trying to do the same things, each parish could specialise."

"Like...?"

"Like you in St. Olaf's. You're very good with your ministry to primary school children. We in St. Stephen's have a vibrant ministry to young people with our special Sunday night services and youth fellowships. Perhaps the next incumbent in St. Saviour's would be chosen for his or her ministry to the sick, visiting hospitals and nursing homes and looking after the elderly? We could share pulpits on a regular basis, too."

Guy was on a roll. "And maybe one of us could take over primary schools and boards of management, another secondary schools and so on. I'd say you have had your fill of primary schools, eh?"

Not if I got proper support from my superiors, including you! Wendy thought.

"So, what do you think? What is your initial response? I think it could be a super idea and a template for other parts of the diocese, and indeed for the whole Church of Ireland. We'd be pioneers!" Guy rubbed his hands and sat back.

"It's quite a lot to take in," Wendy began.

"Yes, well, off the top of your head..."

"I'm not sure it would work. For a start, you'd have to employ at least one and a half full-time people. That's quite an added expense on parishes that are already being stretched financially. And you'd have to rent office space. It wouldn't be fair to the other parishes if the central office was in one parish's buildings. That might smack of a takeover!"

Guy's smile was fading fast. It was Wendy's turn to get on a roll.

"And then you're going to dilute parishioners' loyalty to their parish, their spiritual homes. They give, often sacrificially, to the ministry and maintenance of *their* parish. I'm not so sure that they would be as generous or as committed to what you call a 'team parish'. The Church, for many people, is their local parish.

"I can see the benefit, maybe, if churches in an area were struggling and needed to pool resources. But not where churches are going well and making ends meet, as the three parishes are doing in Lislea."

"But—" Guy tried to interrupt, but Wendy was going to have her say.

"And another thing—there's the question of churchmanship, since you mention exchanging pulpits and taking each other's services. Your church is charismatic-slash-evangelical. Mine is definitely middle of the road, and at the moment, St. Saviour's is on the high side."

"But I can be high, if needs be," Guy protested. "You should see me in my chasuble, swinging the smoking handbag!"

"But I can't see me, without robes, doing all your stuff with hands in the air!" Wendy said. "I think it's a matter of identity and loyalty, and I don't see these two essentials being strengthened by your proposal. In fact, I think they would be undermined, and the churches themselves weakened. Guy, I'm sorry to disappoint you, but I couldn't back such a scheme, nor do I think would the people of St. Olaf's." *And let you take all my young people into the bargain.* Now wouldn't that play right into the hand of the three amigos—and Laurence Finch!

Clearly disappointed, Guy rose to go. He had lost his customary bouncy affability.

"Oh, by the way." He stopped and looked Wendy in the eye as they reached the front door. "You're on the list to do an assessment of your ministry sometime soon. I'll be in touch to arrange it." And he left, without so much as a thank-you.

Chapter 16

SELECT VESTRY TIME again in St. Olaf's. Wendy paused outside the kitchen of the parish hall wondering if the three amigos were having another pre-meeting session. All seemed quiet, so she headed up the corridor to the committee room.

She signed the minutes of the last meeting. 'Matters Arising' completed, Wendy was just about to move to Item One when Edgar Broadstairs piped up, "Rector, you haven't mentioned what you're going to do regarding the matter I raised at the last meeting about modernising the services to cater for young people. It's in the minutes—" he waved his copy "—and I'd like it to be discussed further."

"I second that!" said Raymond Johnson.

"And so do I," parroted Sam Davidson.

"I think I made the point at the last meeting that liturgy and services are my prerogative," said Wendy. "That remains the case. Now can we move on to the first item on the agenda?"

"Well, it's just that the three of us went to St. Stephen's last Sunday evening, just to see for ourselves the kind of service the archdeacon puts on for young people."

"It wasn't really our scene," Raymond Johnson admitted. "A bit too loud and lively for the likes of me. But there were plenty of young people."

"We were talking to Archdeacon Guy at the end of the service," added Edgar, "and he said he would be delighted for his gospel band to come to St. Olaf's some Sunday evening...if they were invited."

"I've just appointed a new organist, as you know," Wendy replied. "We'll be discussing his remuneration under Item Two of this evening's agenda. Don't you think it's only fair to let him settle in and make his mark?"

As usual, the other members of the Vestry said nothing.

"Let me say that Mr. Wilson has plans for the choir," Wendy continued, "and you may be interested to know that he has been approached by some members of St. Stephen's to join our choir. Obviously, not everyone there is as enthusiastic as you seem to think about the services in the archdeacon's parish. Now, Item One, the sexton, Roger Simpson."

Wendy had inherited a parish sexton, who, in return for a modest wage and accommodation in the sexton's house, was supposed to clean the church and the parish hall, cut the grass around the church, verge for funerals and make sure the heat was on for services and activities in the parish hall.

None of it Roger Simpson did well, if at all. Wendy was always getting complaints from users about how cold and dirty the hall was, and how the toilets badly needed cleaning. Old bits of Christmas and harvest decorations could be seen in various corners of the church, and the grounds were never as tidy and well-kept as they should have been. All Roger Simpson was good at was dressing up in his sexton's gown for services and trying to look important.

In spite of all the grumbling and complaining, nobody, not even the cantankerous Edgar Broadstairs, was prepared to tackle the problem of what to do about the sexton. The honorary treasurer complained that he was a drain on parish finances and pointed out that quite a tidy sum could be made from letting the sexton's house. Rental property was always in demand in Lislea.

But how to get rid of Roger Simpson? His wife suffered from depression and was seldom seen. What a field day the local press would have if the church were to sack him and turf him out of the house!

There was a further issue: it was suspected that he stole some of the Sunday collections before the counters and recorders came in on Monday morning. When the list of free-will envelope contributors was published in the annual parish accounts, there would be complaints from a number of parishioners that their contribution was higher than recorded in the report.

The same old arguments for and against sacking him were rehearsed again. Getting a consensus was impossible. For whatever reason, no one was prepared to grasp the nettle. The honorary secretary said he would investigate the legal position. It was progress of sorts.

Chapter 17

A FORMAL MEETING BETWEEN the nominators for St. Saviour's and Steve was arranged. There was one anomaly—they wanted to meet in St. Patrick's rectory! Harry White was paranoid about people from St. Saviour's finding out who they were considering if the interviews were held in the church. Their hall was always too busy for privacy.

Steve agreed, reckoning that when they saw how bright and modern St. Patrick's rectory was, they would realise how much work would be necessary to make St. Saviour's rectory comfortable and habitable.

But it would mean getting Laura out of the house for the evening. Heaven knew what she might say or do if she met the nominators. Fiona arranged a sleepover for her with one of her friends. Andrew would be all right and would be happy to watch sport on the TV in the family room.

"And, of course, you would like me to bring in coffee, like a good clergy wife?" Fiona said with a little edge to her voice. "I'm not doing tray bakes for them. There will just be bought biscuits. I'm not giving the impression that I'm a clone of Ruby McKeever, the last rector's wife!"

The interview went well—or Steve thought so—an impression confirmed by Harry White, who gave him a wink and a nod as they shook hands to say goodbye. The Board of Nomination was due to meet in two weeks' time.

***

Those two weeks seemed interminable to Steve, and the prospect of a move to St. Saviour's was seldom out of his mind. He found it hard to concentrate on parish work, even though there was plenty he could be doing.

The day of the Board's meeting arrived. Steve knew it was scheduled for four p.m.—should he go out visiting after lunch? What if he got delayed at someone's house? How long would a decision take? Serving in a different diocese, he had found it hard to suss out who else was in for it. Usually when clergy met, vacancies were discussed and gossip shared, but maybe the silence about St. Saviour's was because they all knew he was in for it!

He sat at his desk. He tried to read, tried to pray, drank coffee, watched the clock and repeated the process all over again.

Fiona was at work; Laura and Andrew, with after-school activities, weren't due in from school until later.

When the phone did ring, he jumped in fright, even though he was expecting it!

"This is Bishop Christopher here. Congratulations! You have been unanimously appointed to St. Saviour's. Welcome to Daneford diocese! I'll ring again in the next few days to set a date for your institution service. We'll keep an official announcement quiet until Sunday, when it will be announced in St. Saviour's, and presumably you'll do the same in St. Patrick's. You and Fiona have my best wishes."

It was just after five p.m., and Fiona would be on her way home, so he'd get her on her mobile. Just when he had finished talking to Fiona, Laura and Andrew came in. *Better bite the bullet and tell them the news.*

Laura scowled at Steve. "You never think about me, do you?" Oh, no! I don't count! You never think how it will affect me and my friends or Mum! No, it's all about you!"

Another door slammed. Thankfully, this time, the glass stayed intact. Laura stomped off to her room.

Steve looked at Andrew, who shrugged his shoulders and threw his eyes up to heaven. "Don't worry, she'll get over it. We played a match against Lislea last year. They've got a pretty good rugby team. They beat us hollow! It'll be good."

Good old Andrew, thought Steve, somewhat relieved. At least one of his children was happy with the move.

With the family told, Steve rang a few of his close clergy friends to let them know. He couldn't be sure they wouldn't hear before Sunday. The Church of Ireland was as leaky as a sieve. He'd wait until Saturday evening to let some close friends in the parish know and, of course, his churchwardens.

He didn't know how he felt. Elated yet apprehensive, excited yet fearful. And then the doubts started coming. Would he be up to it?

The phone rang again, jolting him out of his mixed thoughts.

"Hello, Steve! You probably don't know me. I'm Wendy Morris, the rector of St. Olaf's in Lislea. I'm a member of the Board of Nomination that's just appointed you to St. Saviour's. We're going to be neighbours, so first of all, congratulations! And secondly, I was wondering if you and Fiona would like to come over for a meal sometime soon so we can say hello and get to know each other?"

"Well, thank you. Yes, that would be lovely," replied Steve.

"Maybe sometime next week, after all the announcements have been made? I'm free Tuesday or Friday."

"Fiona isn't back from work yet, but I'll check with her and let you know. Thanks again. I look forward to that."

A good omen, at last?

Chapter 18

Telling his parishioners of his forthcoming move to St. Saviour's was more difficult than Steve had imagined. He'd left the announcement until the end of the Sunday morning service, not wanting them to be distracted during the service itself.

They were immediately suspicious when he asked them to be seated after the blessing. He found it hard to keep his emotions in check as he told them of his new appointment, and there was an audible intake of breath when he broke the news.

At the church door after the service, he found it impossible to answer their whys—"But we thought you were happy here!"—and he thought he detected just the slightest note of reproach.

The honorary treasurer's wife, never one for withholding an opinion, arched her eyebrows and, in her usually loud voice, asked Steve, "You're not going through the male menopause and having some kind of mid-life crisis, are you?"

The date for his institution was set for mid-September. The problem was the rectory: there was so much to be done. He was going to have to commute from St. Patrick's and bring Laura and Andrew to their new school.

The following Saturday morning was fixed for Steve and Fiona to meet with Harry White and Norman Bradley, the glebewardens responsible for the rectory and its upkeep.

Norman was a new glebewarden, elected at the last Easter Vestry in March. He was a partner in a firm of architects that was getting a name for itself with many landmark buildings around Lislea and Daneford.

As they opened the door, the rectory looked bare and desolate, and even though it was still warm outside, the house had a cold, damp feeling about it.

"Easy to see this house has been vacant for some time!" Harry got in before Steve or Fiona could mention it. They went through the rectory, and it was agreed that all the rooms needed papering and the woodwork painting. A new kitchen was also agreed.

Norman Bradley was in architectural design mode. "I've been thinking about that window that looks out into the garden from the kitchen. If we're going to put in a new kitchen, then we could put a patio door where the window is and make a paved area outside the kitchen. It would make a lovely outdoor dining area and give direct access to the garden from the kitchen, instead of that side door off the utility room and those two little spare rooms. Would you agree, Harry?"

Harry sounded a cautious note. "Yes, it would be ideal—if we can get the treasurer to find the funds."

A slight niggle of doubt flitted past Steve's mind. He hoped Harry White was not all talk and no action. "While we're in the kitchen, can we look at those two small rooms off the utility? There doesn't seem to be a study per se in the main house. I was thinking that if those two little rooms were made into one room, it would be an ideal study-cum-rectory office. They are right beside the side door, giving a separate entrance, and there's also a separate toilet." Steve was thinking of how well that arrangement worked in St. Patrick's.

They went to investigate.

"That is a capital idea and very easy to do," Norman enthused. "An RSJ would need to be fitted, but very little else would need to be done. A great idea!" He beamed at Steve.

"Could I mention about the main bedroom?" Fiona asked as they gathered again in the kitchen. "There's no en-suite, just a wash-hand basin. The bathroom is at the other end of the landing, and the toilet is halfway down the stairs."

They went upstairs to have a closer look. The landing was the whole width of the house with the main bedroom separated from the bathroom by three other bedrooms. "I wouldn't want a visiting preacher to be embarrassed by seeing Laura and me rushing down the landing for a shower!" She hoped that might lighten the request.

"Yes, yes, I see your point," Norman said, looking around the vast bedroom. "There's certainly space for an en-suite."

"Isn't there usually a problem with upstairs showers in old houses? asked Harry. "I've seen them causing damp patches in the rooms below them."

"No, not now," Norman replied, already measuring up where it might be installed. "The new sealing compounds are very watertight. It shouldn't be a problem. It's all very possible." He looked at his watch. "I'm due on the golf course in an hour's time. Is there anything else we need to discuss?"

"Yes, there is one more thing," Steve said, as he looked around the well-worn and faded squares of carpet that were left in all the rooms. "What about carpets? When we moved into St. Patrick's rectory, the house was fully carpeted. They came with the house. We have none at all to bring to St. Saviour's. I realise that the parish is only obliged to carpet public areas and a guest bedroom, but could that remit be extended? We would greatly appreciate it."

"I don't see why not!" Norman replied.

Harry White was more cautious. "We will certainly make a case for that when the Select Vestry meets next week. What may happen is that we will give you a budget for carpets and let you choose them yourselves."

Norman was in a hurry. "I'm going to have to go. But I will draw up a list of works and try to have estimates for next week's meeting. Good to meet you both!" And he was gone.

As they were leaving, Harry gave Steve a set of keys for the rectory. "You may want to have another look around on your own. I know there's a lot to be done, but I can assure you that Norman and I will do our utmost at the Select Vestry meeting next week to get it all passed. I'll let you know as soon as I can."

Again, Steve had that flicker of concern. Was Harry White being less than optimistic about what the Vestry would agree to do?

Chapter 19

Ian Wilson, St. Olaf's new organist, drove up to Wendy's rectory.

"You're well secluded here," he remarked as she opened the door. "All those big trees behind that wall must keep the sun off the front of the house."

"They certainly do. You only have to look at all the moss on the tarmac." She pointed to the damp carpet of green over much of the front of the house. "And the driveway can be pretty dark at night. That's why I leave the gates open. I can drive straight up to the front door. I've reported the broken streetlight, but nothing has happened so far. Anyway, come into the study. It's on the bright side of the house."

Their discussion progressed well, and Wendy could sense that their ideas and expectations generally matched. It would be a good partnership, she felt, without the tension and difficulties she'd had with Cedric Selby. As their meeting came to a close, they agreed to meet at least once a month to plan the music for services.

"Of course, my wife Jane will be joining the choir. She has quite a good voice, if I can say it without bias!" Ian laughed. "Maybe you could come round for a meal sometime soon. She's a good cook as well. There's just the two of us, plus a few cats! I hope you're not allergic to them?"

"No, not at all," Wendy said. "I thought of getting a dog, for company and some protection, but I'm out a lot, and it doesn't seem fair to leave a dog alone for long periods. And then there's all the training of a pup. Although it would make me get out and walk more!"

"Before I go…" Ian stood up and collected his notebook. "I thought I should mention that I bumped into Laurence Finch in Lislea the other day. He invited me into Kate's for a cup of coffee. I thought he might want to talk about some school service he was planning. I was mistaken!"

"Oh?"

"I gather he's not exactly a fan of yours! In fact, he wanted to warn me that you could be a difficult person to work with. Now, I've known Laurence for a number of years. Our children went to St. Olaf's school for a year or two when we moved here, so I know what he's like. Disagree with him over anything and you're Enemy Number One—or a hundred and one! I've lost count of the number of parents who've fallen out with him. I'm not looking for any information but thought I should just let you know, and that I paid no heed to him. I make up my own mind, always have, and I'm really looking forward to working with you in St. Olaf's."

"Yes, things are a bit difficult with Laurence at the moment, but thanks for letting me know. He's very involved in St. Stephen's and is full of praise for Archdeacon Guy Morgan. He's trying to get a campaign going to modernise the services in St. Olaf's."

"Really?" Ian's voice hinted at his concern.

"Even offered to arrange for the archdeacon's praise band, or whatever he calls it, to play in St. Olaf's."

"Really?" Ian repeated.

"Some members of the Select Vestry want to buy a drum kit to go in the sanctuary," Wendy continued, but seeing the look of horror on Ian's face, quickly added, "Only joking! But

I'm not keen to have St. Saviour's praise band here, unless you want them?"

"Me? Definitely not! I had enough of praise bands in churches in the North. No, those twang gangs are definitely not my scene!"

"Nor mine!" said Wendy. They went to the door. "I must say, I look forward to you starting with us on Sunday week."

Chapter 20

SOMETHING FISHY HAS happened. I think you should know about it." Jim O'Keeffe, one of Wendy's churchwardens, rang her early on Tuesday morning. Wendy had had the Sunday off and had spent a few days with her mother on the home farm, helping her to look after her father. She had come home late on Monday night.

"What's it about?" she asked.

"Well, Roger Simpson claims that the church vestry was broken into between the early morning communion and the ten-thirty service on Sunday, and that some free-will envelopes were stolen. But there's no sign of a break-in and he said nothing about it on Sunday."

"Right," said Wendy. "I'll meet you at the church in fifteen minutes."

***

"What's the situation?" asked Wendy as she met Jim O'Keeffe in the church vestry.

"Bob Pearson was on the counting rota yesterday," said Jim. St. Olaf's had a rota of counters who met each Monday morning. They counted the loose collection, opened and recorded the envelopes and lodged the money. The opened envelopes were marked with the amount in them and passed on to the honorary treasurer.

"He was at the eight-a.m. service on Sunday and had put his envelope on the plate. But when he was sorting the envelopes yesterday, his was missing. He looked on the floor and behind the desk but couldn't find it. Roger Simpson was faffing about in the church, and Bob asked him if he knew anything about missing envelopes. It was then that Roger told him the vestry room had been broken into between the two services, and the thief must have stolen some envelopes."

"A likely story!" said Wendy.

"Well, Roger told Bob that when he came to open the church for the ten-thirty service, the main door of the church was open, as was the door to the vestry. He claims that one or two books were scattered around and the drawers in the desk were opened. But as nothing seemed to have been taken, he cleaned up. He didn't bother to mention it to me when I arrived."

"The money and the envelopes are always put in the safe after services," said Wendy.

"Yes, but there's a spare key hidden in the robes cupboard in case one of us forgets to bring ours. Roger Simpson has obviously found out where it hangs."

"I think this is a matter for the police," said Wendy. "Let's meet here at two p.m. with Bob and Roger. I'll call into the station on my way home and see if they can send someone."

Wendy did just that and recounted the story and her suspicions to the duty officer. "There's no sign of a break-in. I think the sexton has been helping himself to some of the collection. There's been suspicions for years, but no proof. Perhaps, if he sees us taking this seriously, he will stop—and start doing a bit of work!"

***

At two p.m., Wendy met the big burly policeman at the church. He inspected the doors and the windows of the vestry room, took notes of Jim's, Bob's and Roger's accounts, and then, in an ominous tone, said, "Now, if you three will kindly leave Mr. Simpson and myself for a few minutes, I have some questions to put to him." He winked at them as they left. Roger blushed with embarrassment.

After a few minutes, Roger and the policeman came out of the vestry to join the others at the front of the church. Roger was a whiter shade of pale and definitely edgy, even more so when a police sergeant and another officer strode up the aisle with great purpose, handcuffs swinging from their belts.

Roger looked at them in fear, his eyes like those of a trapped animal.

"OK! OK! It was me," he blurted. "I took Mr. Pearson's envelope. If I return the money, will you drop this? Look, I'll even resign, I promise, but please no arrest. What will my wife do without me?"

Wendy, Jim and Bob looked at each other, and nodded.

"There will be no charges if you resign. Is that understood?" said Jim, firmly.

"Yes, Mr. O Keefe. Thank you, Reverend Morris. I give you my word."

"And the police are witnesses," added Jim, in case Roger later changed his mind.

Roger shuffled off.

The sergeant looked bemused. "What was all that about?" he asked. "Tom," he addressed Roger's interviewer, "there's been a bit of an incident in the town, and we need everyone to go there. Can you leave this until another day?"

"Sure," said Tom, grinning. "In fact, I think we're finished here, and so is Mr. Simpson! A very satisfactory conclusion, eh?" And off he marched with his colleagues.

Chapter 21

THE ST. SAVIOUR's Select Vestry was meeting under the chairmanship of the Rural Dean, Canon Herbie Cooke.

The enthusiasm and excitement of getting a new rector waned as they began to discuss the refurbishment of the rectory.

Harry White and Norman Bradley had emailed members with the schedule of the proposed works and the estimated costings. Canon Cooke asked Harry and Norman to speak about what needed to be done and why before he opened up the matter to the meeting. Both Harry and Norman spoke in graphic detail about the state of the rectory, which not many members of the Vestry had seen at first hand. The McKeevers didn't operate an open house.

As members took in the scale of what needed doing, Frank Carter, the honorary treasurer and a retired bank manager, didn't waste time in making his contribution. Waving the sheet of works in the air, he declared forcefully, "This is way beyond our means! We can't afford to do all this!"

Canon Cooke, who, as Rural Dean, had been through a number of similar scenarios in newly filled parishes, had also done his homework. Producing a copy of their financial report, he said, "I beg to differ with Mr. Carter. From the figures recorded in your accounts, you can afford to do the repairs and improvements—all of them!"

"We've worked hard to build up our reserves over the years," retorted Frank. "We can't use them all up on the rectory." Looking around at the other members of the Vestry, he went on, "If you remember, the last diocesan architect's report said that at some time in the near future, the church roof is going to need a major repair. Already some of the slates have begun to slip. We must be cautious and careful and keep some money aside for the rainy day which will surely come!"

Longstanding members of the Select Vestry who remembered leaner times, nodded in agreement.

"Wouldn't painting the walls be cheaper than papering?" suggested one.

"Does it really need all this work?" asked a member who had never set foot inside the rectory in the McKeevers' time.

"Sure, we don't ever get the weather for patio doors and sun decks!"

"Why can't the new rector use the church vestry as an office?"

"Canon McKeever managed well."

Like a breach in a dam, the objections to the works became a flood.

The more Harry and Norman talked up the possibilities and potential of the rectory, the more the members of the Vestry feared for their reserves.

Canon Cooke did all that he could to persuade them to be generous, but Frank Carter's dire warnings ruled the day.

"Perhaps our chairman will tell us what the diocesan regulations are concerning what needs to be provided in a rectory," suggested Frank Carter, who had also done his homework.

"The diocesan minimum, and I stress minimum, is that the public areas of the rectory should be carpeted and curtained, and that includes a guest bedroom. And, also, the provision of utilities and appliances in the kitchen," Canon Cooke stated. "These are the minimum. Parishes are asked to be as generous as possible."

"I have no problem in agreeing to all the diocesan requirements, and that is what I propose we do!" Frank Carter declared. "We will do what is lawfully required."

"But we need to do more than that!" Harry White protested. "How many of you have seen the kitchen? It's antiquated! None of us would put up with a kitchen like that in our own houses, and nor would our families! Let's be generous as the diocese recommends. Some of us have seen St. Patrick's rectory where Steve Adams is now. It's comfortable and modern. We can't ask him to move into a house that is substandard by any yardstick."

"It served the McKeevers well, and they never complained," countered Frank. "They made it very comfortable. I've been there. Why can't the Adams do the same?"

Norman Bradley did his best to get the works accepted, but some of the old guard were suspicious of his high-profile firm of architects—'them and their fancy plans!'

In the end, after a lot of debate and discussion, and in spite of the best efforts of Canon Cooke and the glebewardens, the Select Vestry agreed to the diocesan minimum requirements, plus a new kitchen.

Chapter 22

STEVE AND FIONA had been back to see St. Saviour's rectory and had brought along Fiona's mother, who was anxious to see where they would be living. She was not impressed, to put it mildly!

"Of course, Steve, you'll make them do a complete overhaul, won't you?" She fixed him with one of her mother-in-law stares, which made him quake. "After all, it's only what Fiona and the children deserve. Look at the lovely house you're making them move from."

Oh God, it's all going to be my fault, thought Steve with a sinking feeling. *I'll never hear the end of it if St. Saviour's don't come up with the goods.*

The excitement of the move was turning to anxiety. Fiona had also been aware of Harry White's note of caution when they viewed the rectory the previous Saturday morning. Was he rowing back on the works they had suggested?

As they waited to hear from Harry, Fiona started to suffer from migraines, a sure sign of stress. Steve was waking earlier than usual in the morning, his mind in turmoil with a brooding premonition of trouble to come.

All they could do was wait.

***

It was Saturday morning. St. Saviour's Select Vestry had met the previous night. Steve was at his study desk, trying to compose a sermon. It was not going well.

Harry White rang Steve. He was not his chipper self. He sounded deflated and defeated.

"I'll come straight to the point," he said. "The Select Vestry met last night, and despite the best efforts of Norman and myself, and Canon Cooke—the Rural Dean— I'm sorry to say that not all the works we discussed will be done. We tried very hard but were overruled by financial considerations."

"Oh, that is very disappointing. So, what exactly are they going to do?" asked Steve as Fiona brought in two mugs of coffee. He beckoned her over to listen.

"Yes, it is disappointing, and I'm bloody furious!" They could hear the anger and embarrassment in Harry's voice. "In the end, and it was a long meeting, the Select Vestry agreed to put in a new kitchen, but to meet only the diocesan requirements for the rest of the house."

"Which are?"

"Redecoration, carpets in public areas including a guest bedroom, and white goods."

"So, no en-suite in the main bedroom, no new study-cum-office, no patio doors and very limited carpeting?"

"That's it, I'm afraid," said Harry. "It was nothing personal against you and Fiona. It was all to do with money. Our treasurer, Frank Carter, put the fear of God into the members about the possibility of needing a new church roof, quoting a quinquennial report, and although the money is there to do all the work we talked about last Saturday, he persuaded the Vestry to keep as much as possible aside for the roof. I am really very, very sorry, but Norman and I were outvoted."

Fiona sat down and put her hand to her head, which had begun throbbing.

"We will need to meet sometime to decide on paper and paint," Harry said. "Let me know when you and Fiona are free." And with that he rang off.

Steve put the phone down and looked at Fiona and saw the tears on her cheeks. What was he to do? He was due to meet the bishop on Monday morning. Should he just put a stop to the whole process now and tell the bishop he was withdrawing from the appointment? Had it all been a terrible mistake? Had Laura been right all along? Had he let ambition rule his heart above his family?

He sat beside Fiona and put his arm around her. They sat in silence for some minutes.

"I...*we* have got some serious thinking to do over the weekend," Steve said. His heart was breaking at what the Select Vestry's decision was doing to Fiona. "This is becoming a horrible mess. I'm going to have to tell the bishop on Monday if it's on or if it's all off, and to tell the truth, I think it's going to be the latter. I think we've had enough!"

Chapter 23

WENDY DROVE UP the driveway to the rectory and was immediately suspicious. The front door was open, and as she got out of the car, she could hear the burglar alarm ringing inside.

She had been at a lunchtime meeting of the deanery clergy. It was only two-thirty p.m.

She got out of the car and tentatively entered the rectory. The outside alarm cut itself off after twenty minutes, so she reckoned that whoever had broken in had already left. She took out her phone and rang the police, realising as she did so that it would have been more sensible to do that before she entered the house.

She went to the cupboard under the stairs where she had put her father's rifle. If the intruder was still in the house, the sight of the rifle might frighten him off and save her from being attacked.

She opened the cupboard, felt around for the gun, but it was gone, along with the boxes of ammunition.

She next moved to her study. It was a complete mess. Books lay scattered on the floor—presumably, the burglar had thought that something valuable might be hidden behind them. Drawers had been opened and emptied, and there was a pile of pens, Pritt sticks, markers and paperclips around her desk.

The same chaos met her in the kitchen and in the bedrooms.

Apart from her father's rifle and boxes of cartridges, the only other items that appeared to be missing were pieces of jewellery that her grandmother had left her.

She kept no money in the house, though the way that the hot press and jars in kitchen cupboards had been emptied indicated these were the usual places people hid cash and valuables.

The police arrived quickly. Their first action was to give Wendy a telling-off for entering the house and not waiting for them. "We could have been calling for an ambulance—or a hearse," they told her sternly.

"You're very secluded here," they remarked, looking around. "High walls and no neighbours. An ideal property to break into! And what about the big house next door?"

"Oh, there's nobody ever in there. At least, not that I've noticed."

"And is the alarm connected to a monitoring service?" asked one of the officers.

"The church has talked about that, but it's one of those things they never got round to. Probably too late now. Like closing the stable door after the horse has bolted!"

"Well, it's still worth doing."

Wendy was told not to tidy up until someone arrived to dust for fingerprints, but the police didn't hold out much hope that a culprit would be found.

What did interest them was the rifle and the boxes of cartridges that had been stolen.

"How does a lady of the cloth come to have such a weapon in her possession? And where is your gun licence?"

Wendy explained about her father's Alzheimer's and her mother's worries. The police were not impressed.

"You should have deposited it in the police station for safe-keeping," they admonished. "It was very foolish, and against the law, for you to have an unlicensed gun on the premises."

After the fingerprinting, including Wendy's, had been done, she set about the unenviable task of tidying up.

Chapter 24

NEWS TRAVELS FAST in parishes! The report of the burglary made its way around the community at the speed of light. As phone calls came in to check Wendy was all right, she ruefully thought of how hard it was to get people to respond to a request for volunteers when something had to be done.

One of the first to ring her was Ian Wilson. No doubt his policeman's nose for trouble was still twitching. He insisted that Wendy should come over for something to eat that evening. There would be plenty of time for her to clear up tomorrow. He would be round to collect her in an hour's time, so she could have a drink with her meal. He and Jane would not take no for an answer, but Wendy readily agreed. She could do with a bit of company after the day's events. And anyway, she had still to meet Jane socially.

Jane was also from Northern Ireland. Although brought up in Dungannon, a provincial town in Co. Tyrone, she had moved to Belfast to train as a nurse in the City Hospital and had met Ian through mutual friends.

In her early sixties, the same age as Ian, Jane was of medium height, slim and trim, with close-cropped grey hair. She had an attractive, pleasant, friendly face, but Wendy couldn't help noticing that she looked tense and stressed.

Jane and Ian had prepared lasagne accompanied with their homemade garlic bread, which was delicious. "I'm sure you won't object to a wee glass or two of wine after all you've been through today!" Ian said as he opened a bottle. "Don't worry—I'll stick with water so I can take you home later, although you're more than welcome to stay!"

They talked about the break-in, with Ian saying how difficult it was to catch those who committed petty larceny, although the fact that a rifle was stolen made it more serious.

"You would have fitted into the North very well," Ian joked. "When I was on the beat in some of the areas along the so-called Peace Line, nearly every second house had a rifle stashed away!"

They talked about the North, and Wendy, who, unlike many of her fellow clergy, had never served in a curacy north of the border, was given an insight into the bitter religious and political divisions and the stressful nature of daily life.

"What about the churches during The Troubles?" she asked.

"Sometimes they contributed to the divisions, but not all of them. The ones who tried to heal divisions never got much support and were often regarded with suspicion. I remember when one curate on the Shankill Road held forth about loving our enemies. He was told to preach the Gospel instead of talking about love! It would be funny if it wasn't so sad."

Ian went on to talk about his local church. "My own rector tried to open up conversations between Protestants and Catholics in the local area. But when it came to the bit, neither side was prepared to meet. He was treated with great suspicion by the ultra-loyalists in the parish. 'Ecumenism', if it existed at all, meant cooperating with the Presbyterians, and that was difficult enough at times. There was so much rivalry between the two churches, and so much jealousy when one succeeded more than the other."

They talked about his work in the RUC and the stress levels, particularly on spouses. Police were targets for attack both on and off duty.

"I suppose you've noticed my limp?" he said to Wendy. "I got caught in an ambush in a Republican area. We were answering a domestic incident call. I was the first out of the Land Rover and was caught in sniper fire. My bulletproof vest saved my upper body, but I was hit in the right leg. The police then moved me to a desk job, which I stayed at until I retired."

Wendy asked how they found life south of the border.

"It's been good on the whole," Jane answered. "People have been friendly and kind. My sister, Ruth, still lives in Dungannon, where we grew up, but it's not that far away, and we visit each other regularly. Everything was just as we hoped until..." She looked at Ian uncertainly. "You may remember a terrible accident just outside Lislea a couple of months ago when a young girl was killed?"

"Yes, if I remember rightly, she had just got off a bus. She walked into the road from the front of the bus and into the path of an oncoming car. The driver of the car was completely exonerated."

"Well, the driver of that car was Jane," Ian said, reaching out to take Jane's hand in his. "She was passing the bus, which had pulled over at a bus stop, when the girl walked straight into Jane's path. She hadn't a chance of avoiding her. The bus driver saw it all happen and confirmed it was the girl's fault."

"Oh, goodness, I am sorry," Wendy said, understanding in a moment why Jane was so tense and anxious. "It must have been an awful experience!"

"Yes. I still have problems sleeping. Still ask myself if I couldn't have been more careful. If I had spent just a few more minutes with my friend in the coffee shop, I wouldn't have been driving past the bus at that moment." Tears trickled down Jane's face.

"And it's not just what happened on that day," Ian continued as Jane wiped her eyes with her serviette. "It's all that has happened since. The girl's family blame Jane for the death of their daughter—their 'princess', as they call her. And even though Jane was cleared of any responsibility, the family have been sending abusive and threatening messages, saying they will make her pay dearly for the distress she has caused them and that they will make her suffer as they have. The girl was an only child, and of course they're devastated, but it doesn't justify the hate mail."

"Have you been to the police about it?" asked Wendy.

"Yes, the police have visited them and warned them. But they come from a large family with lots of connections in the area, and it's not always easy to say who's responsible for the threats. It's a family that also has connections with the criminal world."

"I was in Lislea the other week," Jane said. "I knew I was being followed, and when I looked back, there was this very unsavoury character a few yards behind me. He grinned at me and then slid his finger across his throat and disappeared up a side street. It was so unnerving, worse than I ever experienced in the North, even during the worst of The Troubles. You just don't know when one of them is around. The police have been helpful, but they can't be with me twenty-four hours, nor can Ian."

Wendy could see the haunted look in Jane's eyes, the burden of guilt, fear and anxiety she and Ian were carrying. It made her realise that her burglary was nothing compared to what the Wilsons were going through.

Chapter 25

FACEBOOK WAS BUZZING!

The *Lislea Gazette*, the local rag, had carried a short article and photo of the new curate for St. Stephen's, the Revd. Simon Appleford, looking all innocent in his robes outside the cathedral on the day of his ordination.

Out of courtesy, and also to boast, Guy had intended to tell Wendy about the appointment when he met her to discuss his plan for a 'team parish' in Lislea. But when Wendy had poured a considerable bucketful of cold water on his proposal, he had been annoyed and decided to let her find out when the public announcement was made. Instead, he reminded her of her forthcoming assessment of the past year's ministry. He'd put her through her paces then!

Young (twenty-four), single and handsome, Simon's photo had been shared on Facebook hundreds of times with admirers getting very excited about his good looks. Comments ranged from 'Gorgeous!' and 'Hot!' to 'Just had a sudden urge to go to confession!' and 'I'm sure St. Stephen's will see a sudden surge in attendance now!'

The Ven. Guy Morgan, rector of St. Stephen's and Simon's boss, was delighted at the publicity his church was getting, even when the remarks were not so complimentary like 'Sad to see a guy his age who believes he has an imaginary friend!' Then there were the pious members of St. Stephen's who responded, pedantically 'A man of God is not there to give people the "hots", and anyone who goes to church for that reason should hang their head in

71

shame!' and 'Let's pray he gets sinners to repent and accept Jesus as their Lord and Saviour.'

But one message that really annoyed Guy was 'Maybe he'll attract more than the six over-eighties that usually go to church.' That really stung, especially as Guy was trying hard to get a name for himself as the one who was attracting 'the youth'— that perennial and elusive section of the population who rarely attended church.

One posting had a scantily clad image of Eve offering an apple to Adam, Photoshopped with Simon's face, headed 'Temptation Awaits at St. Stephen's!'

Simon Appleford had grown up in a strict, churchgoing family in Northern Ireland. A member of The Scripture Union in school and the Christian Union in university, he had never kicked over the traces. In the Church of Ireland Theological Institute in Dublin, where he trained for ministry and was appointed Head Student in his final year, he was never among those who frequently gathered in 'The Vestry', the snug in the local pub. He was more likely to be found in a prayer group back in the Institute praying for those who were seeking alternative spiritual support in the pub.

At the annual Christmas Party and Cabaret, an often raucous occasion in the Institute, one of the students sang about Simon:

> I am the very model of a modern Evangelical,
>
> I've information missional, homiletical and biblical,
>
> I know the kings of Judah and I quote the creeds historical
>
> From Apostles to Athanasian, in order categorical;
>
> I'm very well acquainted, too, with matters theological,

I understand the doctrines of the centuries
quadratical,
About the Global Anglicans I'm teeming with a lot
o' news,
And those with liberal attitudes I am very keen to
disabuse.
Oh, I am the very model of a modern Evangelical!

But how was he going to fare outside the rarefied atmosphere
of a theological college in the increasingly liberal and secular
society of a modern republic? And how was he going to deal
with the many young ladies who were beginning to set their eyes
on him?

Chapter 26

STEVE AND FIONA slept little that Saturday night.

On Sunday morning, Steve went over to the church to take the eight-a.m. communion service with the choice he had to make hanging heavily on his mind. There were usually just a few regulars at the early morning service. There was no music and no sermon, only the familiar words of the BCP, and Steve often found it a time of reflection and assurance, a special time to bring before God what was bothering and troubling him.

He came back for breakfast after the service with a firm conviction that, for the sake of his family—and himself—he should withdraw from his appointment to St. Saviour's. Feeling bitter and disappointed with his new congregation was no way to begin a ministry.

He would tell the bishop of his decision when he met him the following morning, and he'd have to go cap in hand to the people of St. Patrick's and tell them that he was staying after all. He hoped they would take it kindly.

The following morning, the bishop's secretary, Louise Roberts, showed him into the bishop's office.

"Let's cut to the chase!" Bishop Christopher said after greeting Steve and showing him to an easy chair while he sat in another one. "I imagine you've got quite a lot on your mind. Herbie Cooke, the Rural Dean, rang me after Friday night's Select Vestry meeting, and it's an understatement to say that I was shocked, annoyed and disappointed at their decision about what to do with the rectory. I have also been in touch with Harry White, whom I know quite well, to hear his side of the story."

Steve decided to say nothing and hear the bishop out.

"Herbie Cooke brought me over St. Saviour's set of accounts on Saturday morning, and I discovered that it is one of the wealthier parishes in Daneford diocese. As luck would have it, I had no pressing engagement for Sunday morning, so I decided I would take their morning service and sent word to the honorary secretary to ask Vestry members to meet me after the service— in the rectory.

"Let's say that it wasn't a wasted visit. I can't promise that everything that was suggested by the glebewardens will be done, like patio doors from the kitchen to the garden. But, in addition to a new kitchen, they have agreed to put an en-suite in the main bedroom, to convert the two rooms at the back door into a study-cum-office, and I persuaded them to allocate a fair sum for carpets and curtains. I think, with careful choices, that all the rooms could be done."

"I don't know what to say!" Steve was very impressed with the new bishop of Daneford.

"I'm hoping that you will say everything is now all right and we can start to plan a date for your institution," the bishop said with a smile.

"Well, truthfully, I was going to tell you I was withdrawing my name. The whole experience has been a bit bruising for both Fiona and me. We were devastated when Harry White told us of the Select Vestry's decisions, especially as the week before, the glebewardens were suggesting improvements we hadn't even asked for. I felt it wasn't a way to start a new ministry in a parish and that it would be better to call it off before it went any further."

"Perhaps I should tell you that most of the opposition to doing the work came from one person, the honorary treasurer, who seemed to exercise an undue influence. You know what select vestries can be like. And it was purely financial, not personal. I must say that I detected very warm feelings towards you as the prospective rector of St. Saviour's.

"So, can I ask you to reflect on all this before making any final decision? Have a chat with Fiona about the changed situation and let me know. But, if you can, don't leave it too long. I would like to strike while the iron is still hot and get the necessary works done in the rectory."

"I'll be in touch with you by tomorrow, at the latest," Steve said. "Thank you. I really appreciate your care and concern."

"Not at all," replied Bishop Christopher, showing Steve to the door. "I hope your response will be in the affirmative."

Louise brought the bishop a cup of coffee. He had some time before his next appointment. Time to remember a similar situation in his own ministry. Interested in hospital ministry, he had applied, and been appointed to a parish associated with a large hospital. Then the fun and games started as he was told that the annual parish fête was *always* held in the rectory garden and in the rectory itself. The Vestry *always* met in the rectory dining room; the Mothers' Union *always* met in the sitting room.

The rectory was situated in the same grounds as the church and the hall, and when Christopher asked for the entrance to the house to be fenced off for privacy, his request was flatly refused, as were any repairs and refurbishment to the rectory itself. His wife's health began to deteriorate, and the doctor put it down to worry and stress. The final straw came when Christopher rang one of the glebewardens to try and sort things out, and he was told that his call was inconvenient, as the glebewarden was on his way to the hall to put out the mats for the Bowls Club.

Christopher withdrew his name and vowed that if he ever became an archdeacon or a bishop, he would make sure that none of his clergy, or their partners, would have to go through a similar experience.

He had kept his vow. Besides, his wife, Pat, would never forgive him if he knowingly let one of his clergy families go through the hell they had experienced.

Chapter 27

Fiona had taken the Monday morning off. She knew how difficult it was going to be for Steve to tell the bishop he was withdrawing from the nomination, and she wanted to be there for him when he came home.

When Steve returned, he didn't look as stressed and strained as Fiona had expected. There was even a bounce to his step. Was he that relieved that it was over?

"The coffee is ready, and I've some sticky buns to go with it. How did it go?"

"Not at all as I expected."

"Was the bishop awkward about it? You don't look as if he gave you a dressing down."

"Far from it! He was extremely understanding. And you'll never guess what he did yesterday—he actually went and took the service in St. Saviour's, met the Vestry afterwards in the rectory and gave *them* a dressing down!"

Fiona carried the coffee and buns to the kitchen table. "Now give me all the gory details."

Steve recounted his conversation with Bishop Hawkesworth.

"And...? Fiona waited.

"Before I left, he asked me to reconsider and to let the appointment stand. I told him that we had both been very hurt by the experience, but we would discuss it again and let him know. He was surprisingly sympathetic, almost as if he had gone through something similar himself."

"So, we have another decision to make?"

"Yes, I think—well, I know he would like an answer pretty soon. Said he would like to 'strike while the iron is hot' and keep the St. Saviour's Select Vestry on the backfoot and get the refurbishment done as quickly as possible."

"But do you think that the Vestry will have it in for you because they were made to change their minds and spend their money? You know what bearpits some select vestries can be!"

"I know Harry White and Norman Bradley and the other nominators will support me. I gather from the bishop that most of the opposition just came from their treasurer, Frank Carter."

Steve's phone pinged, and he took it out to look at the message. He read it to Fiona.

> *My name is Digby Beere, and I am honorary secretary of St. Saviour's Vestry. Bishop Hawkesworth visited the parish yesterday and had a meeting with us after the service. He put us right in no uncertain manner! I just want you to know that in spite of our previous decision, you have the support and prayers of the vast majority of the Vestry and, I am sure, of the whole parish, who are looking forward to welcoming you, Fiona, Laura and Andrew to St. Saviour's.*

The phone pinged again. This time, it was from Harry White saying that all of the works for refurbishing the rectory were going ahead, apart from the patio doors in the kitchen.

> *I hope the hasty decision of the Select Vestry last week will not put you off coming to St. Saviour's. I can assure you that you and your family will be warmly welcomed.*

Steve said nothing. He wasn't going to force the issue, but Fiona knew what answer he was hoping for. They sat in silence for a while.

"Either way, it's going to be a big step," Steve said finally. "I mean, either going to St. Saviour's or telling the people in St. Patrick's I'm not leaving after all. That's going to need a lot of explanation, and will they feel sort of second best? I'm going to have to go to my bishop cap in hand as well."

"Hmm, I hadn't thought of that."

"So...?" Steve looked at Fiona.

"If you hadn't heard from Harry White and the secretary in St. Saviour's, I would have been doubtful. But, well, now it sounds a little more hopeful and positive, and the bishop seems a good guy—unlike the last one! You've already told the parish here, so, if you're prepared to say yes, so am I."

Relieved, Steve took Fiona into his arms.

Chapter 28

Back in St. Olaf's, another rather chastened and guilty Select Vestry met shortly after Wendy's break-in, realising that they should have been more proactive about security in the rectory.

As Wendy told Jim O'Keeffe, one of the churchwardens, who also had her round for a meal, it wasn't the theft of her grandmother's jewellery—she said nothing about her father's rifle—that affected her so much as the sense of having been violated in some way by the burglary. Someone had invaded her private space and had been through her clothes and personal possessions.

And in a way that she hadn't before, she felt vulnerable.

Since being ordained twelve years ago, she had lived in a variety of church houses on her own. Her first curatage had been a small, terraced house on the main street of a village. The front door opened right onto the street, and there was a tiny backyard. Surrounded by takeaways, betting shops and pubs, she had never felt lonely. On the contrary, she longed for a bit of peace and quiet, especially at weekends.

Her second church house, as a priest-in-charge, was in a modern housing estate. There was only one road into the development, once the grounds of an old abbey. But, like branches growing out from the trunk of the tree, all the side roads were off the one main road, which ran the length of the estate. There was Abbey Green, Abbey Avenue, Abbey Lane, Abbey Path, Abbey Close...

Abbey everything! It was nearly impossible to find exactly where someone lived. But there had been no break-ins. Most burglars wouldn't be able to find their way out!

Before Wendy could move to the first item on the agenda, one of the glebewardens apologised for the tardiness of the Select Vestry in having the rectory alarm monitored and for their failure to put in security lighting along the driveway and around the house. "If the alarm had been monitored, a response team would have got there quickly. In fact, some thieves wait to see if an alarm is monitored before entering a property. And we need to illuminate the drive and the area around the house."

It was passed unanimously. Not even the three amigos said anything.

The next item on the agenda was the sexton's house, now vacated by Roger Simpson, as he had promised.

The other glebewarden reported on the state of the house. "It's a shocking mess. Roger and his wife were far from houseproud, and that's putting it mildly! The place stinks. The carpets are only fit to be thrown out. Cupboards are broken, and the paintwork yellowed. It needs a complete overhaul before it can be rented."

At last, the Vestry had something to get its teeth into. Which they did at length, agreeing, in that most Anglican way, that a sub-committee be appointed to draw up a schedule of works!

"Has anyone seen or heard of Roger Simpson?" Wendy asked.

"We're not sure where he's living," one of the members ventured, "but I heard he's still in Lislea."

"And he's been quite vocal about how badly he's been treated by the church," Edgar Broadstairs reported, adding, "He feels that the rector set him up!"

As Wendy was putting away her papers, Jim O'Keefe came up to her. "I don't want to alarm you, but a few times recently when

I passed the rectory, I saw Roger Simpson hanging around the entrance. I hope he's not going to become a nuisance. If you ever find him inside the gate, call the police. We need to move quickly on those security measures."

Roger Simpson's loitering around the rectory entrance wasn't exactly what Wendy wanted to hear, especially as the evenings were beginning to close in. She wondered what he was up to.

Chapter 29

WENDY NOTICED THAT her predecessor, William Allen, had begun attending the early morning communion service alone rather than the ten-thirty service along with Cecily.

She had heard that Cecily was becoming more and more forgetful, and more and more of a handful for William.

Wendy rang and offered to bring communion to Cecily at home.

"Yes, thank you, Cecily would love that. And, if you don't mind, could you use the old service? It's what Cecily is familiar with. She doesn't cope with anything new."

Everything was ready for the service when Wendy arrived. A small table was covered with a white cloth beside the chair where Wendy would sit. The Allens sat on the sofa on the other side of the table.

After a little bit of preliminary chit-chat, Wendy began the service, Cecily joining in correctly with the responses.

Has Cecily's condition been grossly exaggerated? Wendy wondered. In conversation after the service was finished, Cecily had stock responses and comments which at first seemed rational and relevant, but then they were repeated over and over again.

Wendy went into the kitchen to wash the communion vessels, while William made tea. It was then that she saw the plethora of yellow 'stick-its' on walls and cupboards, and the list of important numbers beside the phone extension. She realised there had been no exaggeration about Cecily's forgetfulness.

"I'm afraid Cecily's condition has deteriorated," William said, indicating all the reminders. "I daren't leave her out of sight for long, and if I need to go out, I have to get someone to come in to be with her. That's why I've started going to the early service. It's only half an hour, and Cecily is still in bed and often asleep. I'm a sound sleeper, always have been, but Cecily doesn't sleep much during the night and is often wandering around the house."

Wendy noticed that William had lost weight. His face had become lined with care, and he cut a tragic and pathetic figure. They were both a far cry from the formidable clergy couple who had run St. Olaf's for thirty years.

"How are you coping?" Wendy asked.

"It's been an awful strain. I don't mind admitting it. She gets everything mixed up now. Puts cornflakes in the teapot and all sorts of crazy combinations. At first, it seemed funny, but when it's done repeatedly, it becomes irritating, and I find myself losing my temper with her."

"Would you like me to contact Meals on Wheels? At least that would relieve you of some of the burden of preparing meals."

"That would be a great help. The doctor is putting social services in touch. Cecily watches television a lot, but I'm not sure she takes anything in. And in her more lucid moments, when we try to have a conversation, she can't recall words and names, which makes her frustrated and angry, and she gives up.

"And she has begun to wander. Just the other morning while I was making breakfast, she wandered out onto the street in her dressing gown, and a neighbour had to bring her home. It's all very distressing, especially when, for all of our lives, she was the organised one.

"I suppose I will have to think of a nursing home for her, but they are so expensive! Although Dr. Grant left this house to the church, I still have a small rent to pay—though nothing like what it should be—so perhaps with my savings and State aid and Pension Board help, that will be the next step."

They went back into the sitting room. Cecily had forgotten who Wendy was. "Is this the new curate, dear?" she asked William.

Chapter 30

I HAVE HAD THE most awful dust-up with Laurence Finch!" Ian was meeting with Wendy in her study for one of their monthly planning meetings. "You'd better be prepared for a verbal onslaught from him when you're next in school."

"What happened?" Wendy asked.

"Well, you obviously know they're planning the school harvest service?"

"Yes. The date has been set, but I'm usually presented with the order of service on the morning itself. It's one of Laurence Finch's little displays of authority. I know I'm usually down to give a short talk—not that I'm asked in advance—so I have to be prepared for that. But the school picks the hymns and the songs for the school choir and the poems and the prayers. But you know all that. You've been playing at those services for years!"

"That's just the point!" said Ian. "When Laurence Finch phoned me, I thought it was to give me the list of hymns he wanted played and to arrange a rehearsal for the school choir."

"And it wasn't?" Wendy was puzzled.

"No! It certainly wasn't!" replied Ian angrily. "You know he's enthralled with the new twang gang they have in St. Stephen's? Thinks there's nothing like them. They're the answer to all the church's problems?"

"Tell me about it," said Wendy. "I've had it from all angles, including his three supporters on the Select Vestry. Let me guess—he wants them at the school harvest?"

"You got it in one! First, I think it's because he perceives that I'm on your side now, and it's a way of getting at both of us. And second, he's cast himself into the role of recruiting agent for St. Stephen's, especially among the older children in the school. 'They need to see how lively church can be' were his exact words, and then he told me I wouldn't be needed, as one of the praise band could also play the organ."

"And what did you say?"

"I told him that as I'm the organist in St. Olaf's, no one is playing the organ without my permission. End of story! In fact, just to let you know, I will be locking the organ in case he didn't hear correctly."

"Well, he didn't discuss it with me—not that he ever would!" added Wendy.

"So, be prepared to be slagged off when you are next in school. But nobody is going to play the organ in St. Olaf's without my say-so! Over my dead body! In fact," Ian smiled ruefully, "those were the very words I used to Laurence Finch. I spent years as a policeman in the North checking for explosives under my car. Do you think I should start doing the same in Lislea?"

Seeing Wendy's worried face, he laughed, "Only joking!"

Wendy hadn't realised how dogged Ian could be. Beneath a very affable and agreeable manner, there ran an obstinate streak.

"Oh, and one other thing for you to store away in your memory when dealing with Laurence Finch. Jane and I went to the theatre the other night in Dublin. When we were walking back to the car park, we saw Laurence Finch and some other man coming out of a rather dubious establishment—The Sunset Strip Gentlemen's Club! It's a glorified strip joint!" Ian laughed.

Wendy gasped, but she was intrigued. "Did he see you?"

"I think he did because he very quickly turned into a side street. He wouldn't like either you or me knowing about that! Maybe that was behind my sacking as organist for the school harvest."

Where will all this end? wondered Wendy. Laurence Finch was a formidable foe.

Chapter 31

WENDY WAS WOKEN from a deep sleep by a chorus of sirens as a fire brigade and an ambulance screamed past the gates of the rectory. She rubbed her eyes and looked at the clock. It was three in the morning.

They stopped not far away, and Wendy could see their strobe lights flashing through the bedroom curtains.

She crawled sleepily out of bed and went to the window to see if she could identify where the fire brigade had stopped.

She was astonished to see flames leaping skywards and smoke billowing in large clouds from a house in the next road. Another fire tender roared past the rectory, followed by a police car, their penetrating sirens piercing the quietness of the night.

She was still trying to identify exactly where the fire was when the phone beside the bed rang.

"Reverend Morris? You don't know me, but I live opposite Canon Allen and his wife, Cecily," said a rather breathless voice. "Their house is on fire. The fire crew have got one of them out, but I don't know which of them it is. I thought you would want to know."

"Yes, yes, thank you. I'll get over there right away." Wendy jumped into her clericals and rushed out.

Already a group of neighbours had gathered, their concerned and shocked faces illuminated by the flashing red and blue lights of the police and emergency services.

Wendy approached a police officer, explaining who she was.

"It's not looking good for the old couple, Reverend, though they managed to get the husband out alive. He's suffering from some burns and smoke inhalation, but they reckon he should be all right."

"And his wife?" Wendy asked anxiously.

"I'm sorry to say she didn't make it," the policeman replied. "She was cooking something on the stove. But why she was doing that as this hour, I don't know."

"She had Alzheimer's, and quite advanced at that."

"Well, that explains it. But it was too late to save her when the emergency services got here. The whole kitchen was an inferno, and it spread quickly. Her husband couldn't get down the stairs—he was rescued from an upstairs window."

"Where is he now? Can I see him?" asked Wendy. "I was with him and Cecily only yesterday."

"I'm afraid not. He's been taken to the hospital."

Slowly, the fire was brought under control, and it was confirmed that the likely cause of the fire was the cooker, as two knobs on the stove were found on the full position.

A collective gasp was audible as a black body bag was stretchered out and put into the second ambulance.

Wendy rushed back to the rectory, got into her car and drove to the hospital. There was little she could do except say a brief prayer with William and let him know she was there.

The next morning, she rang Bishop Christopher to inform him of what had happened. "Poor William Allen was probably so exhausted looking after Cecily that he didn't know she had gone down to the kitchen. I imagine she thought it was dinner time. It's all so sad. He was really at the end of his tether and completely worn out looking after Cecily—and himself. I brought them communion the other day, and he was beginning to accept that Cecily would have to go into a nursing home. He's going to need somewhere to stay when he gets out of hospital. They had no children, and Cecily's sister lives in England. The house is a complete wreck."

"Let me know when you think it would be appropriate for me to visit him in the hospital," Bishop Christopher said.

"I'm planning to go in again this afternoon—I'll give you a call afterwards."

"Thank you. Take care of yourself, Wendy. I know you've had a lot to put up with recently, and I want you to know you have my support. I was planning to have a chat with you sometime soon, and I will. Thank you for all that you're doing."

Tears came to Wendy's eyes. Support at last! What a contrast to Bishop Arthur Easterby. The last time she had spoken to him, she had also cried—but out of anger.

And now to the school harvest!

Chapter 32

THIRTY MINUTES BEFORE the service was due to begin, Wendy went into the church. Laurence Finch was fussing around with microphones which were screeching with feedback. He refused to ask for help and turned his back on Wendy when she approached. In his mind, she had put Ian Wilson up to refusing permission for the organ to be used.

The ear-shattering feedback continued. The band's sound system and the church's were obviously not compatible and were feeding off each other. The praise band, who had positioned themselves at the front of the nave, moved as far away from the church microphones as they could, but it made no difference.

Embarrassingly, parents were beginning to arrive, and little ones put hands over their ears.

One of the teachers, dispatched by Laurence Finch, came up to Wendy. "Mr. Finch says you're to adjust the church's sound system to stop the feedback!" Wendy waited, eyebrows raised. "Please!" said the teacher and scuttled back to her red-faced, vein-throbbing principal.

The usual levels on the amplifier controls had white Tipp-Ex marks opposite them, so re-adjusting the microphones would be no problem. Wendy lowered the levels until the feedback stopped. The teacher returned with the order of service, and Wendy saw that she was down to do the introduction and the blessing, and— just as well she came prepared—a short address.

The noise had abated. The band had tuned their guitars; the drummer had loosened his wrists with a few drum rolls. They were ready to begin.

With the church amplifier on very low, Wendy knew she would have to project her voice to be heard. But how were the children going to manage?

The first child was to read a poem of welcome. Everyone strained to hear. Her class teacher made signs to her to raise her voice, making the child so nervous that she promptly got sick.

If there was one thing Wendy remembered from lectures on children's ministry in Theological College, it was, for children's services, to have a bag of sawdust, a roll of kitchen towel, a bucket and a shovel ready for such eventualities.

Sprinting from the vestry, Wendy mopped up the mess, which had luckily landed on a tiled part of the floor. The school staff froze in their seats until her class teacher led the little girl out for some fresh air.

Laurence Finch, now near apoplectic, signalled for the music group to sing the first song. St. Stephen's was a far bigger church than St. Olaf's, which they hadn't take into account. Again, children put their hands over their ears while the parents looked horrified. The bass notes throbbed and thumped throughout the building. It was turning out to be a disaster. Wendy tried turning up the volume as much as she could without causing feedback again, but still the children couldn't be heard. Unfortunately, the St. Stephen's band could!

Wendy thought Laurence Finch was going to have a stroke. Teachers and pupils left by a side door. Pity them for the rest of the day!

Wendy did her best to smile at the main door as parents left. It was no use trying to explain that the praise band were not her idea. She just had to grin and bear it—and not let it happen again.

As she cleaned up the remains of the vomit, Laurence Finch stood over her and snarled, "You'll pay for this, sabotaging my service! And so will Ian Wilson!"

Which was worse? Wendy wondered. *Actual bile or verbal bile?*

Chapter 33

AFTER LUNCH, WENDY went to the hospital to see William Allen. She was surprised to find him quite alert, even though his arms and hands were swathed in bandages and he wore an oxygen mask.

He brushed aside any concern for his injuries. They were nothing compared to losing Cecily.

"I hadn't realised she had got out of bed. I was sound asleep. I didn't know she was trying to cook something. She'd lost all sense of time. I didn't even smell that something was burning. If only I'd woken up before it was too late!" Tears ran down his cheeks. He turned to face Wendy. "We'll have to talk about Cecily's funeral."

"Let's not worry about that just yet," said Wendy. "We can defer it until you're fit enough to attend. I'll talk to the funeral directors if you like."

"Would you? I'd be so grateful. But I don't want to leave it too long. I haven't slept since coming into hospital, so I've had time to think. What I would really like is to have her funeral on All Saints' Day. That would be in a week's time. It would have been our diamond wedding anniversary. Do you think that would be possible?"

"Yes, I'm sure that can be arranged. What a lovely idea—both for personal and theological reasons. We can have it after the ten-thirty service that day, but there's plenty of time to organise the details."

"And one other thing," William said. "Cecily loved St. Olaf's Church, as I do too. What I would really like is for her remains to be received into the church the night before, so she could rest overnight in the place that meant so much to her..." William broke down, and Wendy could barely make out "...for the last time."

"Of course." She reached out and took his hand. "Try not to upset yourself too much. We'll do it just as you wish. We'll talk more about it in the coming days."

There would be lots to talk about apart from the funeral, Wendy realised. Where was William going to live while the house was being repaired? Would he even be fit enough to go back there on his own?

"As you know," William said, having recovered some of his composure, "we didn't have children, and we don't have close family apart from Cecily's sister. She lives in the Midlands of England. It's a little village called Sudbury, in Derbyshire. Her name is Emily Robinson. I don't recall her number, and I'm sure the phone book was destroyed in the fire, but I would want to let her know."

"I'll contact her if you like. I'll look up Crockford's, find out who the vicar of Sudbury is and ask him or her to get me her number."

"The vicar should know, for she is a regular church attender and involved in her local church. Just explain why I can't do it myself." He looked at Wendy, tears in his eyes. "You are a very kind lady, thank you."

"Now you get some rest, and I'll call in again tomorrow afternoon. Oh, by the way, Bishop Hawkesworth would like to come and visit you. Shall I tell him that would be all right?"

"Yes, please do. Whenever suits him."

William was getting very tired, so after a short prayer, Wendy left.

What a day! she said to herself, driving home in the car. At least there were no meetings that evening. Then she remembered. She had invited the Adams for a meal, and she had nothing prepared.

Chapter 34

As Steve and Fiona stood outside the front door of St. Olaf's rectory, a van, emblazoned 'The Mandarin Express', drove up at speed and a young man emerged with a pile of polystyrene boxes.

"Ah, I see I am caught red-handed!" Wendy laughed, as she took in the boxes. "Come on in! I'm afraid I've had one of those days. I was going to cook something, but I didn't get home until after five, and there was only time to do a tidy-up! I hope you're OK with Chinese?"

"It's one of our favourites," said Fiona. "Actually, I'm not much of a cook myself, so it's a frequent fallback."

Steve handed Wendy two bottles of wine. "I don't know if you prefer white or red, so here's one of each. I hope you do drink wine?"

"Is the Pope a Catholic?" laughed Wendy. "Here, let me take your coats and come into the sitting room. I'll put these boxes in the oven to keep warm. Would you like a glass of wine, or a gin and tonic, or a whiskey?"

"Gin and tonic would be lovely, but make mine very weak. I'll be driving home," Steve replied.

The sitting room was bright and airy with French doors opening onto the garden at the side of the house.

Fiona nudged Steve. "Pity they're not putting doors like that into St. Saviour's!"

"Welcome to Lislea!" Wendy returned from the kitchen and handed them their drinks and sat down in one of the armchairs.

"This seems a nice rectory," remarked Fiona.

"Yes. It's OK once you get into the house. It's very overshadowed at the front with all those tall trees in Chalfont overhanging the wall. And the driveway can be a bit dark and spooky, especially on a winter's night. I had a burglary the other week, and the Select Vestry has promised to instal security lights along the drive and around the house—that should happen in the next few weeks. I can't get the council to repair the streetlight at the gate, which would help a bit. But otherwise, the house is fine. I hear they're going to do quite a bit of work in St. Saviour's rectory. Can't say it doesn't need it! It was very old-fashioned and basic the last time I was in it with the McKeevers."

"You can say that again!" Fiona said with a grimace. "However, after a decidedly choppy start, most of what is needed is going to be done."

"Thanks to Bishop Christopher," Steve added, "and not the treasurer of the Select Vestry, Frank Carter. If it wasn't for the bishop's intervention, I'd have withdrawn my application."

Steve and Fiona gave Wendy a brief résumé of their trials and travails with the refurbishment of St. Saviour's rectory, and of Bishop Christopher's intervention.

"Yes, I'm impressed with our new bishop," Wendy said. "He seems in touch and has the good of his clergy at heart. Not like the last one!"

"Don't mention Arthur Easterby!" said Steve. "He snookered my chances for St. Saviour's the first time around. Didn't want me in the diocese and so delayed the appointment until it reverted to him!"

"I'm only a new diocesan nominator, so I wasn't on the Board for that. But I heard the rumours. Arthur Easterby was a selfish, ambitious bully. I had my own run-ins with him too. Although... I wouldn't have wished for him and Sarah to die as they did— Oh my gosh! The Chinese! It's time we ate. I hope it's OK with a plate on your knees. Let's keep it simple! And Fiona, what about wine? Red or white?"

The conversation flowed, each feeling they could trust the other and become friends as well as neighbours, and it was nearly midnight when Steve and Fiona left Wendy to drive home. Steve was relieved that he had stuck with soft drinks all night, apart from the very weak gin and tonic at the start of the evening.

Chapter 35

THE BUILDERS HAD moved into St. Saviour's rectory. Steve and Fiona drove over to meet the foreman and to check on the plans. They didn't doubt that Harry White would have all in hand...but just to be sure.

As Steve was chatting to the foreman and going over the schedule of work to be done in the kitchen, there was a knock on the front door. "I'll go and answer that," said Fiona.

Standing on the doorstep was a woman, petite and blonde, of an indeterminate age, dressed in what Fiona could only describe as a floaty, hippy-type outfit.

"Hello, Fiona," she said, stretching out her hand. "Oh, I may call you Fiona, mayn't I? I'm Eva Jackson, and I'm the enrolling member of St. Saviour's Mothers' Union. I was just passing, and seeing a strange car and the builder's van, I thought it might be you and Steve coming over to inspect the work. So, I just want to say 'hello' and welcome you to St. Saviour's."

"That's really kind of you," said Fiona. "I can't ask you in. As you can see, the builders are everywhere!"

"Don't worry." Eva smiled. "We're all looking forward to having a young couple and children in the rectory. Poor Canon McKeever and Ruby—we loved them both deeply, but they were getting on and weren't as active in the parish and the wider community as they should have been, or, I should say, as they would have wished to be."

Fiona began to suspect this was more than a welcome call.

"I know our members are looking forward to being able to meet again in the rectory—and to see all the refurbishments!" Eva smiled with her lips, but her eyes were challenging. Fiona was momentarily, not lost for words, but unsure whether to say what was in her mind at this first meeting with a parishioner of their new parish.

Before Fiona could respond, Eva Jackson continued, "We meet every first Tuesday afternoon. The stacking chairs must be in the garage. We only use the kitchen to make tea. We have a box with our own cups and plates. We leave them in the utility room, out of your way!" There was that false smile again, but this time, Fiona didn't miss a beat.

"Well, Mrs. Jackson, I'm not sure that arrangement can continue. For one, I am a working wife and not at home during the day. For two, Steve is always out, and three, we have two teenage children who will have the run of the house. And I am not a member of the Mothers' Union and have no intention of becoming one!"

"Oh dear, how disappointing—on both counts. The members really looked forward to their afternoon in the rectory. I suppose we could meet in the parish hall, but it won't be as cosy and comfortable, and most of our members are getting on. Maybe we can change your mind about becoming a member!" Again, that sickly smile.

"Oh! There is just one other matter I wanted to mention." Eva Jackson was not one to be deterred. Fiona braced herself for another onslaught.

"I also organise Meals on Wheels in Lislea. It's quite a demanding role, but I take our Lord's command to love one another very seriously, and we are all called to make some sacrifices." She looked at Fiona accusingly, daring her to disagree. "There's a little chorus the children sometimes sing in church— 'Love is something if you give it away, you end up by having more'. Well, that's certainly been my experience, as it is yours, I'm sure, as a rector's wife."

Dear God, what's coming next? Fiona steeled herself.

"We're short of cooks at the moment, and I was hoping you might join our loving group. You say you work full-time, but maybe on your day off, even as a driver?"

"Look, Mrs. Jackson, we haven't moved into the rectory yet, and heaven knows when it will be ready. But even when we do, I'm afraid that the answer to both your requests is in the negative. Apart from the fact that I am a rotten cook, we will have a lot of adjusting to do. Now, if you don't mind, I really have to go."

But Eva Jackson was not to be put off. "We won't give up hope just yet! I mentioned to the girls in Meals on Wheels that I would approach you. They'll be so disappointed!"

I'm not giving in to blackmail, thought Fiona, getting angrier by the second.

"My brother is ordained, a returned missionary, and seeing all my sister-in-law does, I just thought you would welcome being part of the community from day one," Eva said accusingly, adding, "We've heard such good things about your husband!"

Fiona stifled an expletive, saying instead, "I've got to go!" and started to close the door.

"Oh! If you ever want a listening ear, just call me. I think I have a special understanding of the strains of clerical life."

Eva Jackson floated off in her floaty clothes. Fiona leaned against the inside of the front door. The expletive she had been stifling emerged loud and clear, startling the painter, who didn't think he would hear such language in a church house.

Chapter 36

HALLOWE'EN—A TIME OF fun for many children as they dressed up and went round the neighbourhood trick-or-treating.

Wendy remembered how, as a child, she would come home on Hallowe'en night loaded with sweets and nuts after having called at neighbours' doors. There would be games like 'bite the apple' where the apple would be suspended on a string from a rafter or trying to retrieve money with her mouth from a basin full of water.

It had been such innocent fun back then. But recently, she'd felt that Hallowe'en had become a bit more sinister. Was it because Christianity was waning in adherence and influence? Hallowe'en—All Hallows' Eve—was a Christian festival but had been introduced to try and Christianise the old pagan festival of Samhain.

Samhain celebrated the end of one year and the beginning of another. It marked the end of summer and the approach of winter. According to legend, it was the time when spirits were released from the underworld to do mischief. It was a time when all the normal rules of behaviour were overturned and when people lit bonfires as a protection against evil spirits.

Yes, innocent tricks, or *fairly* innocent tricks were played on people at Hallowe'en. Wendy remembered some of her neighbours in the country disassembling the horse-drawn cart of a single man who went to the pub every night. While he was away having a drink—or two—they reassembled the cart in the man's kitchen—"Just for fun!"

No doubt the kids who pelted people's houses with eggs thought it was 'fun' too, but it was hardly innocent or harmless anymore. The previous evening, she had seen a young person fire a rocket at a man walking his dog, and she feared for some of her elderly parishioners, who would have firecrackers or smoke bombs, not to mention stink bombs, dropped through their letterboxes. It seemed to be the night when fireworks were let off. Fireworks were illegal in Ireland but were never in short supply.

And so it was that the remains of Cecily Allen arrived at St. Olaf's to a cacophony of fireworks exploding around Lislea.

There was just William and a few friends accompanying the coffin. Wendy had managed to contact Cecily's sister, and she, a widow, had come to stay with her brother-in-law. Wendy had found an apartment that would suit William, and the bishop had been able to tap into a charitable fund to help with rent for the short term.

Ian Wilson had offered to play at the beginning and end of the short service to receive the coffin. William had asked for 'Nimrod' and 'Jesu, Joy of Man's Desiring', two of Cecily's favourites.

William looked fragile and frail, even shrunken, in his black overcoat as he leaned on his sister-in-law's arm. Emily Robinson, tall and erect and capable, looked the picture of health. Wendy was relieved that she was able to stay with William for as long as was necessary.

Knowing that the next day's funeral service would be a big occasion, Ian wanted to run over the details of the service. He also wanted to hear all the details of the previous week's school harvest service.

"Come over to the rectory for a cup of coffee," Wendy invited. "I'll fill you in. It wasn't pleasant!" She'd come to hate Hallowe'en night, and it would be good to have company for a while. "You'll have to give me a lift, though. I've been sitting at my desk all day, so I decided to walk to church for a bit of exercise."

"That makes two of us," Ian said. "Jane's taken the car and gone to Dungannon to visit her sister for the night. So, I had to walk to church as well. It won't do me any harm!" He grinned and tapped his tummy.

They set off together, dodging dressed-up children and the occasional firecracker. Dogs howled as fireworks exploded. It was all a bit surreal.

Chapter 37

IAN LEFT THE rectory about ten o'clock. The 'cup of coffee' had become a bottle of wine. "You don't have to worry about driving," Wendy told him, "and you want to hear all about the band from St. Stephen's and their harvest debut in St. Olaf's. It's going to take some time!"

After Ian had left, Wendy finally made coffee. Better to have a clear head in the morning, but it was too early to go to bed, so she switched on the television to catch up with the day's news. Then she would give Paula a late-night call to catch up.

Fireworks continued into the night. Wendy left the curtains open, enjoying the dazzling display of colours in spite of herself.

Usually a sound sleeper, she woke up during the early hours of the morning to more bangs and flashes. Not fireworks, but thunder and lightning. She could hear the rain lashing against her bedroom window and gurgling down the drainpipes. *I hope it clears up for this morning's funeral, or else poor Cecily will be laid in a very watery grave.*

William wanted a burial. He wanted to mark the spot where she was buried with a proper headstone, rather than a marble tablet in the Garden of Remembrance. The grave had been dug the day before, and checking it after it had been dug, Wendy noticed that the base of the grave had been lined with pine branches. At least, she thought as she lay in bed listening to the storm outside, the branches would hide any pools of water in the bottom of the grave.

Wendy stayed in the church after the mid-morning service for All Saints' Day. The rain had continued all through the morning, and she made a cup of coffee for herself in the vestry, half expecting to be joined by Ian Wilson.

The church began filling with people. Wendy met William and his sister-in-law at the door and accompanied them to the front pew. There was no sign of Ian. It wasn't like him to be late for a service, and usually for a funeral, he would start playing as people arrived.

Hurrying back to the vestry, she rang him on her mobile. No answer! Maybe she should have called him when she saw the heavy rain and offered him a lift to the church. But that would have been far too early, as she had a service before the funeral. Hopefully, he was on his way, but he was leaving it terribly tight.

Wendy looked in the cabinet which housed the sound system. *Yes.* As she had hoped, there was a CD from the last funeral. It would have to do until Ian arrived. Luckily, it was a classical piece and not a pop song.

She put on her surplice and stole. She would have to start without Ian. As she came out of the vestry, who should be sitting opposite, but Laurence Finch with a smirk on his face. He must have realised what was going on and was enjoying Wendy's predicament.

Wendy apologised for the non-appearance of the organist. William Allen's face was like thunder, indicating that such a thing would not have happened in his time!

Wendy composed herself and carried on with the service. Her address was sympathetic and comprehensive, and William's face softened.

Silently, she led the cortege out of the church to the adjoining graveyard. As if by a miracle, the rain had stopped, and a feeble, watery sun was trying to shine.

As she made her way along the church path to the grave, the funeral director, Kevin O'Brien came rushing up to her. "Stop, please, don't go any further! We've got a big problem!"

Telling the coffin bearers and William to wait, he took Wendy by the arm to the side of the grave.

"There's a body underneath the pine branches! And it's fresh, not a skeleton. The heavy rain must have washed the clay away. We've got to call the police."

Wendy peered closer. She recognised the clothing. There was no mistaking who it was. He had worn the same jacket and trousers at the rectory the previous night. It was Ian Wilson!

Chapter 38

W HAT WAS WENDY to do? It was not something for which pastoral or liturgical lectures in Theological College prepared you!

Clearly the burial could not continue. Wendy went up to a stunned and puzzled William and Emily. "I'm afraid something has been found in the grave, and it has to be investigated. We'll have to postpone the burial until that has happened."

"What...what do you mean?" William said. And then, sure that his years of ministerial experience would be able to solve any dilemma, he tried to push Wendy aside. "Here, let me have a look!"

But Kevin O'Brien, who was standing beside Wendy, put a restraining hand on William's arm. "Wendy is right, Canon Allen." His tone brooked no discussion. "What we'll do now is we'll take your wife's coffin back to the funeral home until the situation is clarified. I'm sorry, but there's nothing else we can do at this time." In spite of William's protestations, Emily Robinson firmly turned her brother-in-law around and walked him back towards the church.

"Will you or I make some kind of announcement to the mourners?" Kevin asked Wendy.

"I'll do it. I know most of them. You call the police and get them here as soon as possible."

Wendy moved towards the large group of friends who had gathered to say a final goodbye to Cecily Allen. Their puzzlement was palpable. "I'm afraid the burial of Cecily's remains can't continue at this moment. I'm sorry I can't say anything more. Cecily's coffin is being taken back to O'Brien's Funeral Home until we can have a service of burial. Thank you for your support for William and Emily."

As the mourners slowly turned to go home, the wail of police sirens was heard approaching St. Olaf's, adding to the confusion of the mourners, who gaped in astonishment as two police cars swept into the church car park. Six police officers jumped out and hurried over to the grave.

Detective Chief Inspector Frank Mulready introduced himself to Wendy and went over to peer into the grave. Whatever depth of soil had been used to conceal Ian Wilson's body had been washed away by hours of torrential rain. Ian was lying on his back, and his face could be seen clearly through the pine branches.

The police officers returned to their cars and brought a tent to cover the grave. DCI Mulready rang to request the attendance of the police pathologist.

"We're now treating the graveyard as a crime scene, so it's off-limits to everyone. We'll let you know when the postponed burial can take place," the DCI said to Wendy as the officers moved to mark off the graveyard with police tape.

"I've already told the mourners," said Wendy. "Mrs. Allen's remains are going back to the funeral home."

"Good! Now I need to talk to you and the funeral director. Where can we go that will be private?"

"We can go into the church." At least it would be warm.

Chapter 39

As Wendy came out of the vestry, having taken off her robes, DCI Mulready and Kevin O'Brien were deep in conversation in the front pew.

"Ah, Reverend Morris, come and join us," said the DCI. "This is a most unfortunate business altogether."

"Yes, it sure is." Wendy collected a chair from the chancel, placing it in front of the pew in which they were sitting.

"Mr. O'Brien tells me that the person in the grave is known to you?"

"Yes. Our organist, Ian Wilson. He didn't turn up to play at the funeral service this morning, which is most unlike him. Now I understand why."

"When did you last see Mr. Wilson?"

"Last night. Ian played at the service for the reception of the remains of Cecily Allen and then came round to the rectory afterwards to run over the details of today's service."

"What time was that?"

"The reception service was at seven p.m. and only lasted fifteen minutes or so. We both walked back to the rectory, and he left to go home just before ten p.m. I remember the time because after he left, I put on the news. He was walking home because his wife Jane had the car. She was visiting her sister in the North. Oh, goodness!" Wendy put her hand to her mouth. "She won't know anything about this. She's probably been ringing him and getting no reply. I'm not sure what time she was due back. Oh, poor Jane!"

"And did you hear anything suspicious after Mr. Wilson left your house?" the DCI asked.

"I don't think so. It was very noisy. There were lots of fireworks and crackers going off and then the thunder."

"Where did Mr. Wilson live?"

"Just outside Lislea." Wendy gave DCI Mulready the address, realising the discrepancy. "But that's in the opposite direction to the church. He wouldn't have passed here on his way home."

"Did he say he was going anywhere else after leaving your house?"

"No. I just assumed he was walking home. I didn't offer him a lift, as we'd had a few glasses of wine. Anyway, he said he wanted a bit of exercise. There wouldn't have been any reason for him to come back to the church."

"So," DCI Mulready said, "either he came back and was attacked in the church grounds, or else he was attacked somewhere else and then brought to the church and buried in the grave." Turning to Kevin O'Brien, he asked, "When was the grave dug?"

"The day before the funeral. We use some local gravediggers. I inspected the grave when they'd finished, just to be sure they'd dug it to the correct dimensions."

"And what time was that?"

"About three p.m. I was on my way back to the office from a funeral in Daneford Crematorium."

"Did you see anything unusual?"

"No, nothing at all. The gravediggers were just finishing, and they said there had been no problems. I asked them to cut some pine branches to line the base of the grave. It looks a little less stark when the grave is lined."

"I'll need the names and addresses of the gravediggers," said the DCI as his phone buzzed. "Excuse me a moment." He got up and walked towards the back of the church to take the call. A minute later, he was back, his expression more serious than before. "That was the pathologist," he said. "We now know how Mr. Wilson died. He was shot…at very close range."

Chapter 40

As WENDY REELED from the shock, another terrible thought struck her.

"I'm not sure whether you know or not," she said to the DCI, "but a few weeks ago, the rectory was burgled, and a rifle and some boxes of ammunition were stolen—as well as a few pieces of jewellery."

DCI Mulready raised his eyebrows. "A rifle in the rectory? What did you want a rifle for?"

"It wasn't mine. It belonged to my father, who has Alzheimer's. My mother asked me to take it and put it somewhere safe. She was worried in case my father used it and did some damage, either to himself or to others. I did tell the officer who investigated the break-in."

"Was anyone caught for the burglary?" DCI Mulready asked.

"Not as far as I know. There was some suspicion that Roger Simpson, our former caretaker, might have done it. He was seen hanging around the rectory gate a lot. We caught him stealing from church funds, and he resigned before we fired him. I would have thought he had more of a grudge against me than Ian Wilson. Roger blamed me for setting him up."

Kevin O'Brien was listening intently. "Your driveway is very dark. Do you think it might have been mistaken identity?"

Wendy shuddered. "The sooner those security lights are installed the better."

"Assuming for the time being Mr. Wilson was the target," the DCI said, "are you aware of anyone who'd fallen out with him or might hold some sort of grudge?"

Wendy looked hesitantly towards Kevin O'Brien. She didn't want to speak ill of a parishioner.

The funeral director took the hint and stood up. "Well, I've got to be going. I'll say goodbye, Inspector Mulready, Wendy." He nodded to both of them and left.

Once they were alone, Wendy told the DCI, "The only one I can think of is our school principal, Laurence Finch. He'd dropped Ian from playing the organ at the school harvest, and Ian hadn't been too polite about the music group Mr. Finch brought along in his place, although I hardly think that would be a motive for murder. Ian locked the organ and wouldn't give Mr. Finch permission for its use. 'Over my dead body' were the words he used to the principal." Wendy shuddered again, hoping Laurence Finch hadn't taken that literally, but then she remembered what Ian had told her at their last hymn meeting.

"There was one further incident. Ian told me he saw Laurence Finch coming out of a gentleman's club in Dublin. Ian and his wife had been to the theatre, and he thought Mr. Finch saw them getting into their car, as he and another man quickly turned down a side street. That would be hugely embarrassing to Mr. Finch, as principal of our school, if it ever got out. I don't know if it's important, but you might as well know."

"Do you know the name of the club?" asked the DCI.

"It had 'strip' somewhere in its name. Sort of self-explanatory." Wendy smiled ruefully.

"Is Mr. Finch married?" asked Frank Mulready.

"I don't think so. At least, I've never heard of a wife. Even though he's principal of our parish school, I know nothing of his private life—apart from that he's a member of St. Saviour's parish. We never socialised."

"What about your former caretaker, Roger Simpson?"

Wendy recounted the events that led to Roger's resignation. "I'm not sure where he is living now. But, as I said, he's been seen hanging around the gate of the rectory."

"All right. I'll have a chat with Mr. Simpson. Just one more question for you, Reverend. Your father's rifle—do you know what kind it was?"

"I'm afraid not. He used it on the farm, kept it well away from us children. I never really looked at it when my mother gave it to me for safe keeping. He did have a licence for it. Maybe that would have the information you need."

"We can check that out. Now, before I go, is there anything else you can think of that might be relevant?"

Wendy thought for a bit. "Yes, actually there is. Jane, Ian's wife, has been receiving threatening letters and has been followed around Lislea."

DCI Mulready looked interested. "Go on," he said.

"Jane was the driver of the car that killed a young girl some time ago in Lislea. The young girl stepped into the road from the front of a bus, and Jane hadn't a chance of avoiding her."

"I remember the incident," said the DCI.

"Well, it seems that the girl's family have not forgiven Jane, even though she was cleared of any fault. Both Ian and Jane have received hate mail, even death threats."

"Thank you for all your help, Reverend Morris. I'll be in touch."

As DCI Mulready prepared to leave the church, Wendy asked, "What about Jane? Does she know about Ian? Has she arrived home? Is anyone with her? I'd better get across to her."

"She's home, and one of our officers is with her. It would be good if you could go and see her."

Wendy grabbed her coat from the vestry and headed for her car.

Chapter 41

A POLICE CAR WAS parked outside the Wilsons' house, and a female officer opened the door to Wendy.

Seeing Wendy's dog collar, the officer said, "Ah, you must be Reverend Morris. The DCI said you were on your way." She led Wendy into the kitchen, where Jane was nursing a cup of coffee.

"Oh, Jane, I am so sorry!" Wendy embraced her and then sat down beside her.

"I just can't believe it," Jane said through her tears. "We moved from the North to get away from situations like this. How could it happen here?"

"When did you find out?" Wendy asked gently.

"I spoke to Ian just before he left to play at Cecily Allen's reception service. I was going out with my sister. We were having a girls' reunion at a new fancy restaurant in Dungannon. I said it might be late when I got back and not to worry if I didn't ring him to say goodnight. And it was a very late night. It was well after midnight when we got home, and even then, my sister and I stayed up chatting and having a few nightcaps. Needless to say, I didn't wake up too early. I rang him about eleven o'clock, thinking I'd catch him before he left for the funeral. But the line just went dead."

Jane began to sob and took a few moments to regain herself.

"I thought maybe the battery in his phone had run down. He was always forgetting to charge it. I left my sister's shortly after that, thinking I'd be home and have some lunch ready for him after the funeral. I never thought there could be anything wrong.

I wasn't long home when the police arrived. I still can't believe it! Who would do such a thing?"

"Have you contacted the children?" asked Wendy.

"Yes. As you know, they're living in the UK, but they're making arrangements and should be back either tonight or early tomorrow morning. I...I've been asked to identify Ian this afternoon. Would you mind coming with me?" She turned to Wendy with bloodshot eyes.

"Yes, of course!"

"And then the police want to talk to me." Jane's shoulders heaved with sobs as Wendy hugged her and held her close. "My sister's coming later today, but, if you don't mind, could you stay until she arrives?"

"Of course. Anything at all," Wendy assured her.

The doorbell rang, and DCI Frank Mulready entered the kitchen. In a surprisingly gentle voice, he said, "Mrs. Wilson, it's time to go and identify your husband."

***

Later that evening, after Jane's sister had arrived from the North, and Simon, their eldest, had made it home, Wendy returned to the rectory.

Her driveway was sealed off with police tape, and a police officer was guarding the gate.

"Sorry, Reverend Morris, you will have to park your car on the road. The driveway is now a crime scene, and you'll have to put these over your shoes." He handed Wendy a pair of blue plastic slipovers.

As she walked up to her front door, police were combing the driveway. "Over here!" one of them shouted. "I've found a bullet shell!"

Chapter 42

EVEN BEFORE IAN Wilson's murder had reached the late evening news, word had gone around the parish like wildfire, and Wendy's phone never seemed to stop ringing with calls from the concerned and the curious.

Bishop Christopher Hawkesworth insisted he would call round, despite the late hour, and within a short time, he and his wife, Pat, arrived. Pat had made Wendy a large cottage pie that was still warm as she handed it to her. "You have enough on your plate without having to think of cooking, and you mustn't neglect yourself! This should last you a few days."

The bishop, a little guiltily, handed Wendy a bottle of wine. "I know you won't abuse this, but a small glass before bed might help you sleep."

Wendy filled them in on all that had happened and told them about Jane's car accident and the subsequent letters and physical threats. She also told them about keeping her father's rifle and how it had been stolen in her recent break-in. That led on to Roger Simpson, the main suspect for the burglary.

"You've had a lot to contend with recently," remarked the bishop with concern. "All that along with the trouble at school. I've been catching up on the various parochial files," he said, by way of explanation. Wendy decided not to tell him about Ian's falling out with Laurence Finch, in case it might seem that she was being vindictive.

They chatted on for a while about her father and the farm and how her mother was coping. Then he and Pat rose to leave. "If there's anything we can do, just let us know. And I mean that!"

Pat added, "We have plenty of spare rooms in Bishop's House. If you ever feel you need to get out of the rectory, for whatever reason, we can offer you a bed."

Wendy didn't think she ever would but was touched by their genuine concern. It went a long way to restoring her confidence in her bishop as *pastor pastorum*.

Bishop Christopher and Pat pulled on their plastic overshoes. "Are you sure you'll be all right?" Pat asked.

Wendy pointed to the police all around the rectory. "I don't think I will ever be more secure!"

***

The phone rang continuously from early the next morning. The calls were from news reporters looking for interviews. Press photographers were taking pictures of the taped-off rectory gate, and drones buzzed overhead, taking aerial photos.

Reporters rushed towards Wendy as she came out of the gates to go to her car. The police intervened, and Wendy drove off to the church. It also had been taped off, along with the graveyard.

DCI Mulready was talking to a group of officers and turned when he saw her approaching.

"I'm sorry for all this inconvenience. I'm sure we'll have it all cleared up by Sunday. Are there any services planned in the meantime?"

"No. Our midweek service took place before yesterday's funeral, so our next one will be on Sunday."

"Good. That gives us three days."

"How are things going? Am I allowed to ask?"

"I can tell you that we located Roger Simpson and found the rifle and the cache of jewellery. He will be charged with burglary.

We're not sure of his motivation for stealing the rifle and the ammunition. It may be just that they were there or…" He paused. "There may have been a more sinister motivation, seeing that he blames you for losing his position as caretaker. But don't worry, we'll be keeping an eye on him," he said reassuringly, seeing Wendy's concerned look.

"Keep the rifle. I don't want to see it again!"

"The other thing I can tell you is that the bullet that killed Mr. Wilson didn't come from your, or should I say your father's rifle. We found the casing on your driveway. We're pretty sure that's where he was shot. We also found traces of blood."

"There were so many bangs from fireworks and crackers that night, I wouldn't have known if I'd heard a gunshot."

"Well, we haven't yet discovered any tyre tracks apart from your car, though there are lots of footprints near where the bullet was found."

"What about the church car park and the graveside?" Wendy asked

"That's a bit more complicated. The car park is tarmac and used a lot. The graveside is churned up by the gravediggers, plus it was overlaid with artificial grass to hide the clay."

"I still can't believe it!" Wendy shivered.

"We're following up other leads while still examining the graveyard," the DCI went on. "I didn't see any cameras around the rectory, so I presume there's no CCTV?"

"No. The alarm isn't even linked to a monitoring system. Although, like the proverbial stable door, the system is now going to be updated and security lights installed. Even the streetlight might be repaired."

"Yes, your driveway is very dark. A perfect place for a murder," DCI Mulready remarked. "It should have been lit better than it is."

Just then, Wendy's phone buzzed. The archdeacon.

"Wendy, this is Guy Morgan. What a terrible business! How are you coping? Bishop Christopher asked me to keep an eye on you—in the best possible sense, of course—and I was wondering if I could drop over for a cup of coffee?"

Not allowed into the church and not in the frame of mind to work at her desk or even think of a sermon for Sunday, Wendy agreed. After all, pastoral care was being offered, and she had often complained of its lack. Maybe Guy's irrepressible and effervescent good humour and optimism would lift her spirits.

Wendy stopped at a corner shop near the rectory for some milk and biscuits and was delayed as the shopkeeper, whom she knew well, showed her the story on all the front pages of the papers. Then he started fishing, without results, for any inside information.

Wendy's feeling of pastoral support evaporated as she approached home and saw the archdeacon, surrounded by cameras and microphones, holding forth to the press in front of the rectory gates.

Chapter 43

AFTER A FEW questions about how Wendy was coping, Guy Morgan was all talk about his new curate, Simon Appleford. "A super fellow! Was head boy in college. Comes highly recommended. Had the choice of curacies but chose St. Saviour's." And so on, and so on. *Good grief*, thought Wendy, *will 'I, Guy' never go?*

A welcome phone call at lunchtime, when the archdeacon finally left, was from Fiona Adams with an invitation to dinner.

"We thought you might like to get out of Lislea for a few hours. I'm sure it's been non-stop. So, if you'd like to come here for a meal this evening, we'd love to have you over. And there's a spare room if you would like to have a drink and not have to go back to the rectory late at night."

"Thanks, I'd love to! As for staying overnight, that would be too much bother for you."

"Not at all! The bed in the spare room is always made up. See what you think later. Shall we say about seven?"

The invitation cheered Wendy, especially after an hour and a half with Guy Morgan, who had left her feeling exhausted rather than supported by his visit. Having boasted about getting a 'super' curate, he then went on to tell her of all the 'super' things he was doing in St. Stephen's. Wendy counted at least fifty 'supers' in the ninety minutes he was with her, and as many, if not more 'I's. She noticed he didn't revisit his plan for a team parish in Lislea. Perhaps the bishop had also poured cold water on the proposal.

St. Patrick's rectory, although only ten miles away, was in another diocese. Fiona's directions had been clear, and Wendy parked outside the modern bungalow, set in a spacious garden. Two large picture windows looked out onto the garden while a third was at the top of the short driveway set in what once had been a double garage. An arrow pointing right directed visitors to the 'Rectory Office', while a left-pointing arrow indicated 'Front Door'.

"Wow!" said Wendy as Steve opened the front door. "And you're swapping this for that barracks of a rectory in St. Saviour's?"

"Shhh, not too loudly!" Steve put his finger to his lips. "I can't say that hasn't been a matter of some prolonged discussion! Come on in. Dinner is nearly ready, so we'll go straight through to the kitchen." The kitchen was just off the square hallway and was large enough to hold a table, which was set for five.

"We're going to be joined by Laura and Andrew," Steve explained. "Laura is fifteen, going on twenty, and Andrew has just started secondary school. They're both supposed to be doing homework in their rooms. But who knows!"

Fiona came in from the utility room with a dish full of frozen vegetables to put in the microwave.

"Hi, Wendy! Take a seat. It will all be ready in a few minutes. Steve, will you go and call Laura and Andrew to come for dinner?"

Steve introduced the children to Wendy, telling them that she was the rector of the next-door parish to which they were going.

Andrew was broadly built and sporting a bruise over his eye. He saw Wendy looking at it. "I got it at rugby practice this afternoon. I got hit with the boot of a fellow I was tackling!"

Laura was much slimmer than her brother. Her blonde hair was streaked with different colours, and she had studs in her ears.

Surprisingly, she was still wearing her school uniform, if you could call it 'wearing' in the proper sense. Her tie hung halfway down her white shirt, which, in turn, hung over her skirt, which could barely be seen below the hem of her shirt.

Another surprise, especially to Steve and Fiona, was that Laura was so chatty, asking Wendy all about Lislea and 'The Rectory Murder Mystery'!

After dinner, Laura and Andrew disappeared back to their rooms. Steve and Fiona cleared away the dishes, and then the three of them headed for the sitting room. There was a formal dining area off the kitchen, which they went through and down two steps into a large and airy lounge.

"A split-level rectory! How posh!" Wendy exclaimed.

A door in the opposite wall led into another room. "That's my study-cum-office," Steve explained. "The previous owners turned the double garage into a granny flat, so it has its own toilet and an outside door, which is ideal. It was what I finally persuaded them to do in St. Saviour's, knocking the coal shed and garden shed into one."

"An office with an outside door is going to be Steve's legacy in whatever rectory we go to," Fiona said, laughing, then quickly added, "Not that I want too many moves!"

A fire had been lit, the wine had been opened, and they settled easily into each other's company. Wendy filled them in a little more about 'The Rectory Murder Mystery', as Laura had dubbed it, ending up with telling them about that morning's visit of 'super' Archdeacon Guy Morgan, the 'I, Guy'. "He's OK, I suppose, but in very small doses!"

"I had an interview with him as well," said Steve. "He's a bit overpowering. I came out feeling quite inadequate!"

A second bottle of wine was opened. More clergy gossip was shared. It was the first time Wendy had relaxed for quite a few days.

As midnight struck, Fiona said to Wendy, "And you *will* stay the night!"

"I think I'll have to! DCI Mulready might not be so friendly if I was caught over the limit!"

Chapter 44

FRANK MULREADY'S CAR pulled up outside St. Olaf's School, and the DCI made his way to the reception.

"I wonder if it would be possible to have a word with Principal Finch?" he asked.

The school secretary eyed him suspiciously. "Who shall I say is asking, and about what?"

"I'm Detective Chief Inspector Frank Mulready." He showed his warrant card. "It's private business."

The secretary blushed. "Of course! Hold on a moment. I'll see if Mr. Finch is free." She phoned through. "He'll be with you right away."

"Ah, good morning, Inspector Mulready!" Laurence Finch was at his breezy best. "Come on through to my office. Can I offer you some tea or coffee?"

"No thanks, I'm fine."

They sat in his office. Although nowhere near as tall as Frank Mulready, Laurence Finch, behind his desk, seemed to tower over the DCI. And then Frank realised that the chairs in front of the principal's desk were quite low. It gave Laurence Finch both a physical and psychological advantage over those who came to see him.

"How can I help?" ventured Finch.

"I'm here in connection with the murder of Ian Wilson. I understand he was connected with the school."

"He is, or was, a past parent, and he used to play the organ for school services."

129

"When was the last occasion he played for a school service?"

"That would have been the end-of-year service last June."

"Not since then?"

"No. We, eh, changed the format for the harvest celebration and didn't need him."

"Did you discuss the change with Mr. Wilson?"

"Of course! I rang him to discuss the new format. I told him the music group from St. Stephen's—the church which I attend—had offered to lead the service this year, and that he wasn't needed."

"How did Mr. Wilson take that?"

The DCI noticed a vein beginning to throb on the side of Finch's face.

"He may have been a trifle upset, but he seemed to accept it. He's played for school services for many years. Nobody likes change, do they?"

"Would it not be more correct to say that there was an argument between you and Mr. Wilson?" the DCI pressed. "And that threats were made?"

"Certainly not by me! He disagreed with me using the St. Stephen's music group and refused to let anyone play the organ. Ian Wilson could be a difficult man when he wanted." The vein in Laurence Finch's head was throbbing more visibly, and his face was flushed.

"And were the words 'over my dead body' used?" DCI Mulready asked.

Finch became flustered. "They may have been, I really don't remember. But if they were, it was only in a figurative sense. You can't possibly think I am responsible for Ian Wilson's death? That's preposterous!"

If it had been anyone else other than a police officer in front of him, Laurence Finch would no doubt have told them to get out. He was having notable difficulty controlling his temper.

"Mr. Finch, did you see Mr. Wilson in Dublin recently—when you were leaving the Sunset Strip Gentlemen's Club in the company of another person?"

"I… No… I don't know what you are talking about!"

"I think you do. May I ask the name of the man who was with you?"

"I don't recall who it was. Probably just another member making his way to the taxi rank." Laurence Finch blushed. "We don't give away much personal information. It's not that kind of club."

"I suppose not." Frank Mulready paused. "Just one other question. Do you own, have access to or know someone who has a rifle?"

"No! Certainly not! I'm a Christian and an active member of St. Stephen's Church. Check with Archdeacon Morgan."

"Oh, I will," Frank said with a smile. "Can you tell me where you were on the evening of Hallowe'en, Mr. Finch?"

"I was at home. Do you think I was dressed up as a ghoul walking about Lislea?" Finch snapped, getting increasingly tetchy and angry.

"Can anyone vouch for you being at home that evening?"

"Hardly, as I'm not married and live alone. Now, I have more pressing matters to deal with than your fanciful suspicions." Laurence Finch stood. "The school doesn't run on its own! So, if you're finished…" He went to the door and opened it, signifying the end to the meeting.

"I am. For the moment. Thank you, Mr. Finch."

***

After DCI Mulready had gone, Laurence Finch sat down again in his chair, brooding over what had just taken place. He was livid and convinced that Revd. Wendy Morris had set him up. She would pay for this humiliation.

Chapter 45

ONCE MORE, SIRENS pulled Wendy from sleep. Since Ian Wilson's murder, she had tossed and turned most nights, and when she finally did get to sleep, she had horrible dreams in which she was being chased and then fell into Cecily Allen's grave. Last night, she had stayed with the Adams again and had slept soundly. She hoped that the sleepless spell had been broken.

She looked at the bedside clock. Six-thirty a.m. It was just about getting light.

The sirens got closer and closer and stopped outside her gate. She peeped through the curtains of her bedroom. Flashing lights illuminated the roadway. Police were using cutters to get through the gates of Chalfont.

She ran onto the landing but could see no lights on in the big house next door. Police cars drove in through the gates and fanned out in front of the house.

Wendy could make out that the police were armed and wearing bulletproof vests over their uniforms. A helicopter appeared and hovered noisily overhead while training a spotlight on Chalfont. She could see police using a battering ram to break through the front door. Other officers ran around the back of the house.

Wendy quickly dressed and returned to her vantage point on the landing outside her bedroom.

After a few minutes, her doorbell rang. She went down and opened the door to find DCI Mulready on the doorstep.

"You're an early riser!" he said, seeing her fully dressed.

"I'm not usually up quite this early. I think your sirens might have something to do with it." That and the helicopter, which was stationary above them. "Will you come in? The noise is deafening!" Wendy led the DCI into the kitchen. "Coffee?"

"Yes, please. I'm not usually out and about at this hour either."

Wendy put on the percolator and got some mugs from the cupboard. "What's happening next door?" she asked.

"We've had a breakthrough concerning Ian's murder. Ballistics have been able to identify the bullet which killed him. It was from a weapon used in Northern Ireland during The Troubles and has been used since in ambushes and raids. We have good working contacts with the PSNI."

"What's that got to do with Chalfont?"

"We've had our suspicions about the ownership of Chalfont for some time. And then one of our officers discovered a few small CCTV cameras hidden in the trees that overlook your driveway. The wires led into Chalfont."

"Gosh!" exclaimed Wendy. "So, the house next door is owned by terrorists?"

The DCI didn't answer directly but asked, "What can you tell me about who lived there?"

"That's the thing," Wendy said. "Absolutely nothing." She poured the coffee, and they sat at the kitchen table. "It used to belong to the Loftus family, the owners of Lislea Flour Mills, but after Stanley Loftus died, it was sold. Nobody seems to know anything about the new owners. It's supposed to be the headquarters of some group that works with disabled children, but there was never much activity there. Occasionally, cars went in and lights could be seen in the house but never for more than a day or two. I certainly never met anyone who lived there."

"We're still checking through the deeds," the DCI said, "but my theory is that it was bought by terrorists as a money-laundering exercise."

"Oh! I remember Ian telling me something about that. He served in police in the North, as I'm sure you're aware. After he was injured in an ambush, he was investigating illegal paramilitary activities. You don't think…?"

"Yes, I do," Mulready nodded, his expression more serious than Wendy had seen before. "I think someone with a grudge against Ian Wilson followed him to Lislea and has been keeping an eye on him. It was a stroke of good fortune for them when he was appointed organist of St. Olaf's, which meant he would have meetings with you here in the rectory, right beside their base. It was easy to set up the cameras, so they knew exactly when he was here."

"And they chose their night," Wendy said, "when there would be plenty of noise from fireworks."

"An added bonus," the DCI said. "The rifle would have had a silencer fitted, but the fireworks still provided a screen."

"If Canon Allen hadn't insisted his wife's funeral should take place on All Saints' Day, this might never have happened," Wendy mused sadly. "Ian wouldn't have been here, and there would have been no grave to bury him in."

"Oh, it would have happened. If not here, then somewhere else. But the darkness of your driveway and the night it happened worked in their favour."

"I never noticed any lights in the house that night."

"They weren't going to advertise their presence. Anyway, they could monitor the cameras remotely on their phones. They didn't need to actually be in the house."

That made sense, or most of it did. "So, how did he end up in Cecily Allen's grave?"

"Again, they were lucky. They had a van ready at your gateway, and after they shot him coming down your driveway, they carried him to the van. Cecily Allen's funeral was common knowledge around Lislea. They simply took advantage of an open grave in which to dispose of Mr. Wilson's body. They dug the grave a bit deeper and covered him up, replacing the pine branches so no one would notice."

Wendy chuckled without joy. "If not for the torrential rain that night, it might have become a missing person mystery rather than 'The Rectory Murder Mystery'."

"Indeed." DCI Mulready finished his coffee and rose from his chair. "I'll leave you in peace. We're liaising closely with the PSNI and their money-laundering suspects, present and historical. I don't doubt that we'll have the culprits in our sights fairly soon, even if at this moment they're sunning themselves in warmer climes. But we *will* get whoever has done this, sooner or later."

When he reached the front door, he turned to Wendy, "Talking of suspects, I'd steer clear of Laurence Finch for a while. I don't think he was at all pleased to be interviewed about the case, and he may have suspicions about where I got some of my information. He's not a pleasant man, and I don't want another 'Rectory Murder Mystery' to deal with!"

Chapter 46

Wᴇɴᴅʏ's ꜰʀɪᴇɴᴅ, Pᴀᴜʟᴀ Armstrong, was doing lengths in the swimming pool, while Wendy sat on the balcony reading a book. After all that had happened over the previous few months, she needed a holiday before the run-up to Christmas started. Paula had readily agreed to go with her, and they managed to get a last-minute deal in a five-star resort in a little village near Marbella.

The temperature was in the mid-twenties, and they spent their days walking on the beach and lazing by the pool. They hired a car for a few days and explored the nearby villages and pretty harbours. The local village near where they were staying had plenty of eating places dotted around the village square, and each evening they enjoyed being able to eat outdoors and relax over a bottle of wine.

There was even an 'Irish pub' if they got homesick! While preferring the local taverna, they promised to do their patriotic duty and have a Guinness there one evening.

The Irish pub was a popular meeting place and was quite full when, on the last night of their stay, they went for a Guinness after a nourishing dish of paella. A couple left a table by the window as Wendy and Paula arrived, so they made for it quickly.

"This is like praying for a parking space!" laughed Paula, as they sat down and ordered their drinks.

Irish music played softly in the background while many of the patrons were taking part in a pub quiz. Wendy and Paula sat in the window people watching.

"Ah, this is the life!" sighed Wendy. "Away from all the shit of the past few months." She looked at her watch. "I know we have to pack, but it's our last night. Let's have another drink."

Just after their drinks were served, a large BMW screeched to a halt outside the front door of the pub. Two men wearing balaclavas jumped out of the car and rushed to the entrance. Entering the bar, they scanned the patrons, and then focusing on a group of older men in a corner, they aimed their semi-automatic pistols and fired a volley of shots at them. And then they were gone. It was all over in a matter of thirty seconds or less. The BMW took off at speed, its blackened windows hiding any sight of the driver.

As one of the men slumped to the floor with blood pouring from his wounds, the others in the group tried to staunch the flow. They didn't appear to be seriously wounded; the man on the floor seemed to have been the main target. People rushed to get out of the pub and stood in horrified silence in the car park. Wendy and Paula sat glued to their chairs, unable to take their eyes off the carnage in the corner. One of the man's companions was shouting into his mobile phone. Wendy thought she heard him say, "Scotch is dead," but she couldn't be sure. His accent was distinctly Northern Irish.

The barman had phoned for the police, and they arrived with a similar screech of tyres, followed by an ambulance. Paramedics attempted to treat the badly wounded man but after a short while stood back and shook their heads. They treated the minor wounds of his three companions, who were then led away by the police.

More police arrived. The bar was sealed off as a murder scene, awaiting the arrival of the police pathologist. The patrons huddled in the car park. Chairs were brought for them from nearby restaurants, and then began the lengthy job of taking witness statements. At least the night was warm.

It was after two a.m. when Wendy and Paula finally got back to their apartment. They were to be collected by a taxi at nine a.m., so they hastily threw their things into their cases and lay on their beds for a few hours' sleep, if that were possible.

Chapter 47

A WEEK LATER, WENDY got up from her desk to answer the door. She saw from the newly installed CCTV monitor in the hall that it was Detective DCI Frank Mulready.

"I believe you had a rather eventful holiday in Marbella," he said, raising his eyebrows. "You seem to be a magnet for trouble!"

Wendy laughed. "Nothing much escapes your notice. You'd better come in. Coffee?"

"Yes, that would be grand," said Frank. "I thought I might bring you up to date...on both murders!"

"Oh? How are you involved in the murder case in Marbella?"

"We think they're linked, even apart from you!"

Wendy poured two mugs of coffee and put some biscuits on a plate. "Come into the sitting room. I sense an 'are you sitting comfortably' explanation. It all sounds intriguing!"

"What do you know of Ian Wilson's work in the PSNI?" the DCI began as he sat down.

"Not a lot really, apart from what I already told you. I know he was badly injured in an ambush in a Republican area during The Troubles. He was shot in the leg, he said, and he walked with a limp. He was then given a desk job."

"Did he tell you what that entailed?"

"He didn't speak a lot about it. He said it had something to do with investigating illegal paramilitary groups and their goings-on, but he never went into any details."

"Ian and his colleagues were a very successful team of investigators and put many an illegal paramilitary group out of business—and into jail. There was one very big case which involved a high-profile paramilitary boss who ran a fuel-laundering business on both sides of the border. They used a well-secluded farm near the border to extract the red dye from agricultural diesel—which is far cheaper—and then sold the clean product in garages he owned both in Northern Ireland and the Republic. He had petrol pumps all over the place and even a few in Dublin. It was a highly profitable business which earned him millions of euro."

Frank paused to drink some coffee and then continued, "It was Ian's team that caught him. Not only did that result in a hefty prison sentence, but a number of properties he had bought with his illegal gains were also seized by the authorities. The paramilitary leader was known as 'Scotch'. That was his favourite drink."

Wendy gasped. "That was the name of the man who was shot in the Irish Pub! I heard his friend mention it when he rang someone immediately after the shooting."

"When Scotch came out of jail, he vowed revenge on Ian," the DCI said. "Ian had put him away and he had lost his money and his properties. He wasn't going to take that lying down. Ian Wilson was going to pay for what had happened. Scotch was still high up in active paramilitary circles, still with influence."

"And he shot Ian?"

"Not personally. He got some of his foot soldiers to do the job—for a price. But he was behind it. Not all paramilitary arms and ammunition were put out of commission in the Good Friday Agreement. The PSNI have identified the weapon used in Ian's killing to an extreme group run by Scotch."

"But what's the connection with Spain and what happened there?" Wendy was still puzzled.

"When he got out of jail, Scotch didn't go back to fuel laundering. It was too risky, and he was a marked man in that regard. He went into drugs instead—another activity popular with paramilitary groups. But, as you probably know from newspaper reports, there are lots of inter-gang feuds as they fight over areas and profits. Drug traffickers seldom reach old age."

"So, Scotch was a drug baron?"

"Yes. He operated both here and in Spain. But he got too greedy, probably because he lost so much when he was caught fuel laundering. When some of his gang complained a little too loudly about not getting their fair share of the profits from drug trafficking, he had one of them knee-capped as a warning not to challenge him."

"And they took their revenge?"

"That appears to be the case. There's a lot of money in drugs but very little mercy. He's not the first drug baron to be shot in Spain, and probably won't be the last. We're in very close liaison with the Spanish police."

"What about the gunmen who shot Scotch, and the driver of the BMW?"

"The three men who were in the bar with Scotch had their suspicions about who the killers were and passed their names on to the Spanish police. The BMW was found burnt out up in the mountains, but the police raided a luxury villa they suspected was being used by drug traffickers and arrested three men. They sent me footage of the arrest if you'd like to see it."

He handed Wendy his mobile phone, which showed Spanish police pinning a bare-chested man to the ground, handcuffing him, and leading him and two others to a police van. One of the two walked with a pronounced limp.

"As well as the semi-automatics used in the pub, the police found a rifle, which ballistics have since identified as the gun that killed Ian Wilson."

"So, Scotch's own gang turned on him!"

"It seems so," the DCI confirmed. "They obviously had a huge falling out, which led to the knee-capping. Instead of keeping them in order, it led to them killing him."

"There's a kind of rough justice in it, isn't there?" Wendy reflected. "The man who shot Ian in revenge for what he did to him was in turn shot in revenge for what he did to his gang, who may have been the very ones who were contracted to shoot Ian."

"That's the hypothesis we're working on. We hope to charge them with the double murder of two very different characters—a church organist and a drug baron, both linked by the past. Another nugget of information you might be interested in— Scotch's investment in property wasn't confined to houses. He also owned the Sunset Strip Bar in Dublin. We're starting to investigate whether members may have been involved in some of his illegal activities."

Wendy sat back, mesmerised. "You mean…Laurence Finch?"

DCI Frank Mulready smiled and spread out his hands. "I can't possibly comment."

***

A few moments of silence passed as Wendy processed all she had heard, and Frank Mulready thought he heard her exclaim, "Holy shit!" But he couldn't—and wouldn't—swear to it.

About Ted Woods

I am a retired priest of the Church of Ireland, now living in Liverpool.

I served in a number of parishes in Ireland, North and South, most latterly in Rathfarnham, Dublin. I was a General Synod member, a Director of Ordinands, and worked in The Theological College looking after intern deacons in their final year.

For many years, I wrote a column on ministry for the Church of Ireland *Gazette*. For five years before retirement, I wrote a weekly 'soap' – 'Down in St. David's' – for the *Gazette* about the ups and downs of clerical life. On my retirement, another writer took over.

I have self-published a book on Kindle – *And Some There Were...* – a light look at 'the Good, the Bad and the Ugly' in the clergy of the Church of Ireland's past. The book includes twenty-five sketches, historically accurate, of priests and prelates from Reformation times to the twentieth century. With the aim of informing and entertaining, *And Some There Were...* features the rogues as well as the righteous, the murdered and the murdering, priests and bishops alike.

My first novel was *Bishop. Priest* is its sequel.

By the Author

And Some There Were:
Sketches of some Irish Anglican Prelates and Priests

Bishop

Priest